Miriam's Way

Miriam's Way

Cissy Lacks

BEANIE BOOKS

Miriam's Way

Beanie Books
beaniebooksMiriamsWay@gmail.com

ISBN: 978-0-933530-01-0

Library of Congress Control Number: 2013921366

Printed in the United States of America

Miriam's Way

by Cissy Lacks

The story of Miriam Kornitsky,
the main character of *Miriam's Way*,
is based upon true-life experiences
of Miriam (Kenisberg) Poster from
1941 through 1946.

CHAPTER ONE

September 1939
Hitler orders the German army to invade
Poland. Britain and France declare war on
Germany and World War II begins. Two
years later, the Germans complete their
occupation of Poland when they move east
on their way to Russia. Miriam lives in the
countryside of Vilna, Poland.

I t was a warm day in early September when Miriam's father told her he was going to send her away. They had hiked through the Vilna countryside for at least ten kilometers and were on their way home when he stopped her.

"Papa, I'm not tired and we're almost home. We don't have to rest here."

"Miriam, I promised your mother I'd talk to you before we got home today but now we're almost back and I haven't done it."

"Done what, Papa?"

"Talked to you about the war, about what happened to Jacob, and about what's going to happen to us ... and to you."

"What if I don't want to hear, Papa?"

"I'm afraid you have no choice and neither do I."

He put his arm over her shoulder and rubbed it as he talked.

"This countryside you and I love so much is more than beautiful. The black soil is so fertile that crops almost grow by themselves. The Germans want this land and these crops to feed their armies, and they don't care what happens to any of us. You've heard the planes. The soldiers will be in Vilna within days.

"I know you'll take care of me if they come," she answered.

He squeezed his daughter's shoulder so tight it hurt.

"I can't. I couldn't help Jacob, and the Germans are worse than the Russians. They don't like Jews, even pretty little Jewish girls."

He stroked her cheek with his large, calloused hand.

"I'm thirteen, Papa."

"Miriam, I'm afraid for you. Your mother and I have decided to send you away, someplace where you'll be safe. When it's better, in a few days, in a week, you'll come back."

He blurted out the words and just the sound frightened her.

Miriam's father believed in truth. For Nathan Kornitsky, lying to his daughter was an act of bravery, but one that did little to console Miriam.

She only knew she saw her brother Jacob taken away by Russian soldiers and now she was being sent away because of German soldiers. Her brother never returned and no matter what her father said, she knew that he thought she would not return either.

Sometimes, Miriam could get him to change his mind, but this time when she looked at him, he turned away from her. His rejection was worse than the threat of separation.

"Your cousin Sonia is coming tonight and, tomorrow, you'll leave with her."

"No, Papa."

"Miriam, we have no choice."

"Where is Jacob? Can't I go to Jacob?"

"Jacob was strong, like you, and the Russians took him. They needed workers so Russian men could be soldiers. Your mother and I are not going to let the same happen to our other children."

"Why can't Joseph go with me tomorrow? Why can't we all leave together?"

"Because when we return, we'd have no farm. If we have a future together, we must separate now. Don't ask your mother these questions. She can't bear to send you with Sonia, even though we decided we must."

Miriam wanted to cry but she didn't.

That evening supper was a few mouthfuls of bulbous – potatoes cooked with milk – since they had no meat, and some tea without sugar or honey. In the middle of dinner, Nathan leaned both hands on the table and pushed himself to a standing position.

"I've talked to each of you about the war and what it's doing to our family. We aren't sure where Jacob is, and tomorrow Miriam is leaving with Sonia. We are like a herd of sheep grazing in a field when a wolf comes and scatters them. The flock is never the same but it disperses to save itself."

He cleared his throat and ran a finger along the edge of his moustache. His eyes went around the table, stopping to look at each of them.

" I have tried to be a good father to you. At times we didn't have enough food because I wasn't as lucky as some men, but I've done my best.

"I don't have anything to give you but advice. Let your heart guide you and don't fear what it tells you. Be careful of people. Don't go with them, not because they'll harm you, but because they'll be confused. I've taught you to be self-reliant, to respond to nature, and to use your intelligence in a crisis. Count on yourself. Keep your head clear and remember to trust your heart to lead you."

"Yiv vo rachecha adonoi vayishmaracho. Ya air adonoi panov alecha vechunacho. Yesaw adonoi panov alecha veyasame lecha shalom."

"May the Lord bless you and keep you. May the light of the Lord's presence shine upon you and be gracious to you. May the Lord bestow favor upon you and give you peace."

"May we each find our way back. I have nothing more to say."

Miriam's mother, Rebecca, swaying slightly from side to side, started her familiar, almost silent, humming. Nathan sat down and pulled the plate of potatoes toward him, but he couldn't swallow even a mouthful. He left the table to go outside, and Miriam cried the tears she held in all day. Her mother hugged her, but the arms around her only reminded Miriam that tomorrow they wouldn't be there. She pressed herself into her mother's lap and cried harder.

Miriam didn't want to sleep that night and her parents didn't force her. She stayed up as long as she could, and sat

10

before the fire, watching her mother and father as if she'd never see them again. As much as she resisted, she fell asleep on a small rug in front of the fireplace and when she woke, it was to hear her cousin Sonia talking to her father.

They were discussing the safest places to go, deciding together that the forest was the only alternative. Sonia told him about what she saw on her way to the house; refugees filled the streets and roads, making their way toward the East, toward Russia. German soldiers were everywhere. And, even more frightening, she saw two planes flying low over the travelers.

Neither Nathan nor Sonia thought the refugees would make it to Russia. Hiding in the forest seemed to be the only solution. Nathan told Sonia to start on the Vilna-Oshmyany Minsk Road, east toward Russia as everyone else, but they should go into the Rudnicka Forest as soon as they could.

Miriam pretended not to hear but when she could no longer control herself, she shouted as loudly as she could, "I don't want to go."

They turned to look at her, still curled on the rug, tears filling her eyes and her long blonde hair falling over her face. Nathan walked to her and bent down to push the hair from her face. He moved his fingers over her cheeks and rested them on her shoulders.

"Miriam, my only daughter, don't worry. The war won't last for more than a few days and you'll be back."

She wanted to believe him, but the strong pressure of her father's fingers against her cheek belied his reassuring words. From the other side of the room, she heard the low, sad singing of her mother. Her father's repetition of the advice he had delivered several times in the last twenty-four hours did not comfort her.

11

"Miriam, you'll go with your cousin and you'll be all right. You have a horse, a wagon, food and clothes. I know you'll be able to handle any situation because for thirteen years you have been my best student, better than your brothers."

He began to list the things he had taught her, as much for himself as for her.

"You know how important it is to wash, to keep clean; you know what berries and roots to eat if you have to; you can make shoes from leaves and bark; and you can keep warm in the cold.

"Most important, I have taught you to listen to yourself. People will be confused. Don't follow them, follow your heart."

He pressed her hand, kissed her on the forehead and returned to his conversation with Sonia. Hearing that Miriam was awake, her mother stopped her work in the kitchen and came to the fireplace. "Miriam, I want you to wash and look nice." She rubbed her daughter's back as she talked. "First, I'll braid your hair, then you'll take a bath and get dressed."

She brushed Miriam's hair for fifteen minutes until the tangles were out and she could run her fingers smoothly through her hair from the top of her head to her lower back. All the while, she hummed a sad melody Miriam had heard often. The words were even worse, and although her mother didn't sing them, Miriam heard them anyway.

The sky grows dark and overcast.
I seek to walk a different way
Where loving arms will lift me close
And guide a child who's gone astray.

After her mother finished braiding one side of Miriam's hair, Miriam turned to look at her. Rebecca smiled but kept humming. The soft melody was so much a part of her way of handling sadness that she didn't even know she was singing. Miriam would carry this image with her. Her mother was bending over her and they were both surrounded by the familiar sad music of Rebecca's songs.

Sonia didn't talk at the breakfast table. Miriam's two brothers sat across from her and although she would miss them, she already longed for her parents, even though they were still at the table with her.

Nathan told Sonia and Miriam it was time to go. He wanted them to be in the forest before sunrise so that no one could see them on the road, and he thought the way could take three hours. He carried the suitcases to the wagon and asked Miriam to follow. In the dark, she could hardly see her father walking, much less her cousin's horse and cart.

Rebecca turned to her husband, "Nathan, I have my wedding ring in the house. Get it and give it to Miriam." She already gave Miriam her coat. Miriam didn't want to take it because few early September days called for more than a sweater. Her mother said she could bring the coat back, and they would share it over the winter. When Miriam turned to her mother, Rebecca leaned her head on her daughter's shoulder and said, "I love you, Miriam. Don't worry, it's not going to take too long." Then she stroked her daughter's back, and pulled Miriam close. She held her until Nathan came back with the ring.

Nathan told Rebecca to sew the ring into the coat lining and when the ring was hidden in the bottom of the coat, he lifted Miriam up to the wagon seat. She wanted to throw

herself back down into his arms, but she didn't. Her parents
should remember that she was a daughter who listened to
them.

Her father smacked the horse and, as the wagon
started up, he called out, "Guard our ring. It will bring you
good luck. Just remember, you are going to be back with us
soon."

Miriam tried to watch her parents as the wagon pulled
away, but because of the dark, she lost sight of them and of her
house after only a minute. By the time the wagon reached the
outskirts of Vilna, she didn't recognize anything. She began to
cry and, for the first time, her cousin talked to her.

"Miriam, don't worry. We'll just be gone for a few
days. We're only going because the German soldiers are
coming. When they leave, we'll come back home."

Miriam sobbed. The farther they went, the harder she
cried. Finally, Sonia reached over and pulled her younger
cousin toward her. Without both hands directing the horse's
reins, Sonia couldn't prevent the wagon from rocking back
and forth in the holes and ruts of the dirt road, but Miriam's
body stopped shaking only when Sonia held her. In one last
effort, Miriam begged Sonia to turn the cart around and take
them both back to Vilna.

Sonia tightened her grip around Miriam's shoulder but
didn't answer. Miriam wept until she was exhausted, finally
falling asleep on Sonia's lap. Sonia had to shake her to wake
her up. They had pulled off the road and stopped beside a
large lake. The sun was just beginning to rise and in the early
light, Miriam took a good look at her older cousin. She saw
Sonia once or twice a year and talked little with her then,
being so much younger.

Now, she watched Sonia carefully and listened to every word. Sonia was big and healthy looking, even plump. Her long blonde hair, which was braided and pinned against her head, escaped in wispy tendrils everywhere. Her face was red, maybe from working to keep the cart straight on the rough road, and she was talking to the horse as if he were her friend.

"You're very good to us, Lisper, " she said to the horse.

"You earned this drink and a good breakfast too. We're counting on you."

Sonia handed Miriam some food. "Take this to the lake and we'll eat when Lisper does."

She unhitched the horse and took him a few yards to a shallow watering place. While he grazed, they ate too. Miriam asked her cousin questions about the trip.

"Where are we going, Sonia? When will we get there?"

"I don't know Miriam. I only know we must keep going and that once we get in the forest, we'll travel by night and sleep during the day. Day will become night to us and night will become day."

"Why must we do these things? I don't understand."

"Look at old Lisper. See how happy he is with a little grass. He knows that after he eats, he has to pull the wagon, but he doesn't protest. He has no choice so he does what he has to do. We are the same."

"But why must we travel at night? It will be so dark and we won't have any way of knowing where we're going."

"Miriam, do you hear the planes?"

For the first time, she realized she could hardly hear anything else.

15

"Those planes fly during the day and soldiers march during the day. We'll avoid them by traveling at night. Let's hitch up, and I will teach you how to drive so that I can sleep."

When they were on the road to the forest, Miriam started her questions again.

"What is going to happen to us, Sonia?"

"We'll survive. Just do what your father told you."

"But how far can we go?"

"You remember what your father said. Don't ask questions. We'll just keep going."

Miriam grabbed on to old Lisper's reins, as if helping Sonia guide the horse and wagon was notice that she heard her cousin and would stop asking questions. It wasn't until she was holding the reins that she noticed the road was one long path of carts, bicycles, and wagons – and most of them were filled with families. Miriam thought her parents should have left with her, just as these families had done. Almost as soon as Miriam noticed the travelers, Sonia said it was too light to follow the road. They would go into the forest.

Just as on the road, the forest was crowded with people in horse and wagon, but without the faint remnants of the rising sun through the forest opening, it would have been impossible to know people were there. As if their silence was protecting them, no one talked. The only noises were of the wagon wheels and the horses' hoofs hitting the ground. No one talked, that was, except Sonia. She talked all the time to Lisper. "We're depending on you Lisper," she said over and over again, snapping the reins gently.

Miriam and Sonia couldn't stay in the forest all the time because they needed water for Lisper and to bathe themselves. Lakes were outside the forest. When they left the woods, they got off the cart and guided Lisper by hand as if being next to him, rather than on the wagon, would somehow make them less visible.

The first time they crossed the open fields to find water, they saw dead animals, cows and sheep, lying everywhere. They didn't need to hear planes to know they had been there. Cows and sheep were ripped apart from bullets so numerous they could not have been fired from soldiers' rifles. Neither one said what they were thinking and what Miriam had fought to admit. The Germans wanted to kill them and to kill anything that would help keep them alive.

Sonia held on to Lisper, trying to guide him through the carcasses on the ground. She told Miriam to look the other way, but everywhere Miriam looked she saw dead animals. The grass was redder than green and the stench of rotting flesh made her sick to her stomach. She tried walking with her eyes closed, but she tripped over a dead cow. She was lying face to face with it – its eyes open and staring at her, even though it was dead. Right next to it was a cow still alive, making groaning sounds. She thought all the animals were dead. Now, she heard the sound of suffering animals as if it were a plane engine's roar.

The animals still alive had rolled on their sides and were trying to lift their heads, but none could. Their strained efforts didn't bother her as much as the groaning. It started loud and agonizing, then faded, and finally stopped when the animals had no more energy to fight or complain. After some quiet next to her, she knew that one had died. As she walked, she heard groans, then whimpers, then silence.

Miriam asked Sonia to turn around and go back to the woods, but Sonia refused.

"Where there are cows and sheep, there is water," Sonia told her matter of factly. "And the planes have done their job. They won't return soon. We're safe now, and we need the water."

Miriam did not tell her cousin that she saw terror in her eyes.

The next morning, safe in the forest, they heard explosions in the distance. Soon after, a formation of planes flew overhead, followed by another that came low over the trees. With only that short warning, gunfire burst through the trees and onto the open field a short distance away.

The people on the road and in the field were easy targets, but even those in the forest were hit as the bullets came through the trees. For the first time, Miriam heard the screams and groans of dying humans.

"We have to do something. We have to help. We have to," she yelled to Sonia.

But Sonia ignored her. She slapped the reins on Lisper's back, trying to get the wagon away from the chaos. The drone of planes flying over, the staccato sounds of bullets when gunners took aim, and the noise from explosives falling everywhere were not as frightening as what Miriam saw and heard around her. People were wild from fear, running in all directions. Some were screaming, some were crying and some were singing in pleading prayers. Miriam knew the song, "Eli-Eli, lama avatani?" "God, why have you abandoned me?" In a melody she heard only in synagogue, they were begging God not to let them burn and asking God to forgive them anything they had done wrong.

Sonia was talking but Miriam couldn't hear the words over the noise. She was able to make out only one sentence that Sonia kept repeating, "Don't worry, we'll survive."

When the noise from the planes stopped, Sonia pulled on Lisper's reins to slow down the cart. She and Miriam looked at each other, not speaking. Finally, Sonia began as if nothing had happened, "Let's find some berries and nuts and eat our lunch." While they were sitting, Miriam asked questions. She always asked questions even when Sonia wanted her to be quiet.

"They meant to kill us. They flew down over us and shot right into everyone, just like they did with the sheep and cows. Why do they want to kill us?"

"It's better not to think about what just happened, Miriam. It gives us good reason to stay in the forest."

"But Sonia, they killed the animals and now they're killing us."

"The Germans are in Poland," she said. And that is all she said.

Miriam was more frightened than sad.

"How far can we go?"

"We'll go as far as Lisper will take us."

"But can Lisper take us away from all this, and when will we be able to come back?"

"We'll return soon."

It was as if Sonia knew her answers could not give the reassurance she intended. Finished with their meal, the two girls climbed back on the wagon to begin again the steady plodding of horse and cart through the dark forest. The trees were so thick they kept light from entering the forest, even in the daytime, but Sonia and Miriam traveled through the night as well. At sunrise, they saw a little light ahead and knew they were close to the edge of the forest. When they took Lisper out of the forest to drink at a lake, Miriam saw the gold and red colors of the sunrise against the field and in reflections on the water. The beauty comforted her.

While Lisper drank and ate, the girls bathed in the lake and washed their clothes. Miriam's father told them over and over that cleanliness was important. No matter what happened, they were to bathe as often as they could and keep their clothes as clean as they could.

In the quiet of the early morning with the pleasure of the cool water against her body, Miriam almost forgot what she saw the day before. They ate breakfast slowly, deciding to give Lisper a much-needed rest, and then walked the few steps to where their clothes were drying. Together, they hitched the horse to the wagon, and Sonia smiled at Miriam.

They led the horse back to the woods, taking full pleasure from the short walk through the field. As they began, they heard a single plane flying overhead and then short bursts of sharp, cracking sounds. Before they took two more steps, Miriam felt a heaviness leaning against her hands, and she turned to find out why Lisper was pressing so hard against her. She saw blood gurgling from his throat and she watched him drop, rolling over on his side. His eyes were big and his mouth was open – groans coming from it. Miriam stared, her body motionless as if it were frozen to the horse. Sonia shouted, "Run to the forest. Don't stay and look." She pushed Miriam from behind but even as Miriam ran, she heard the groaning subside, and the gasping for air more desperate.

Then the noise of more planes drowned out the sounds of the dying horse.

Back in the forest, they knew they should continue running but neither could move. They lay on the damp forest lawn of decayed pine needles and stared at the treetops. When the plane noise faded, Miriam talked.

"Sonia, they killed Lisper on purpose. He groaned and grasped for air just like those cows. They are going to take everything from us."

"Miriam, Lisper served us well. Forget what you saw and heard. Remember him in front of the cart, pulling us even when he was tired or thirsty. We can get a few things from the cart, but most of our belongings will be too heavy to carry as we walk. But we will be okay without Lisper, good old Lisper."

"I'm tired, Sonia. How can I walk. I can't even see. The forest is so dark. How will we know where to go if we can't even see?"

"We'll be like blind people. In a blind person's mind, she can see everything. Now we must begin to walk because we protect ourselves when we keep moving."

Miriam was lucky to have Sonia with her. Other people were already giving up and going out of the forest to travel on the roads, only to be killed by artillery or bombs. Or else they were captured by the Germans and sent to labor camps. Neither Miriam nor Sonia knew the fate of those who left the forest, but they knew about the bombs and the artillery. Their fears were enough to keep them in the forest. Now, Miriam knew why her parents sent her away; still, she wished she were home with them. At least she had Sonia, and Sonia would tell her what to do.

They traveled a week before they left the forest again. It was hard to stay in the forest when even in the day, the leaves blocked out the sun and created night. Their view had no sky, no mountains, no flowers – all the sights they treasured when walking across a meadow to drink water or wash in a lake.

Finding food was no problem, for early autumn was a good time to be in the woods. Wild berries grew everywhere. Nuts, which had fallen from the trees, were soft and easy to chew because no sun came through to dry them. Nathan taught Miriam what to eat in the woods and she knew there would always be enough. She got the food for her and Sonia.

The two didn't talk much anymore. Sometimes, the noise of planes and bombs made it almost impossible to hear, but that noise wasn't the cause. They didn't want to talk about the hundreds of dead bodies they saw everywhere. In a month, routine became everything. They knew when to walk, when to stop, when to eat, and when to slip out of the woods. Words did not help them in any way.

The trips out of the forest to find drinking water created both pleasure and fear. They enjoyed the brief escape from the forest, a reminder of the outside and a more normal life, but these were also the times most open to attack. Outings were in the daytime because it was the light that guided them out of the forest. They would see a shimmer from the darkness and move toward it, knowing they were walking to the edge of the forest.

The pattern of walking was always the same. Sonia led the way and Miriam followed a few steps behind. They could have walked together but Miriam respected Sonia's age and Sonia protected Miriam. On their sixth trip out, Sonia reached the water, with Miriam her usual five steps behind, when the planes came. As soon as they heard the noise, Sonia turned, frantically looking for a place to hide. But before they could move, the bullets sprayed everywhere. Miriam saw the bullets hit Sonia. She fell, just like Lisper, with her head rolled sideways and her eyes open. When Miriam bent to help her, Sonia rasped with all her strength, "Run to the woods, Miriam. I can't help you."

Miriam bent to touch Sonia's face. Sonia repeated the words, until they were only an imperceptible hiss. A gurgled, choking noise sputtered from her lips and finally voiceless gasps for air.

Miriam could not move as long as Sonia was alive. When she died, no more than a minute or two after she had been hit, Miriam ran back to the forest. She sat on the roots of a huge oak tree and put her arms around its trunk. For an hour, she didn't move or think, only cried. When she stopped crying, it was to listen to what she thought was a voice whispering in the air. She heard her father talking to her.

"Remember to follow your heart and your feelings, no one else's."

The planes were gone. Even the sound of birds, familiarly calling each other across the forest, had disappeared in the aftermath of this last attack. She heard the sound of leaves brushing against one another as the wind gently blew through the trees. Only the conversations of the leaves would accompany her now. She listened to them but she couldn't ask them questions. She thought about going back to see Sonia but she didn't.

Miriam survived, but she was alone. Now, somehow, she would make choices by herself. She got up deliberately and slowly moved her feet in a forward direction, as if she were more robot than human. Her first day alone ended only when she could no longer move. She walked and walked until she couldn't do anything but fall to the ground and escape into sleep.

While she slept, she dreamed. She saw herself with her parents in Vilna, and she heard her father instructing her and her mother singing. When she woke, she could see light at the edge of the trees. Afraid to move until night, she remained hidden and still under the protection of the large oak tree.

CHAPTER TWO

November 1941
For the first time, Germans gas to death
prisoners at Buchenwald labor camp.

T he next day, Miriam talked to the trees – giant oaks soaring up more than 130 feet, linden trees covered with moss, tall red cedars, spruces reaching 160 feet into the sky, and pines whose needles carpeted the forest floor but whose branches grew 125 feet high. When she walked, the hours had no order and the path no direction. She spent the day going from tree to tree, asking what she should do and where she should go. She didn't expect answers from the trees, but she needed to ask questions out loud, hoping that a place deep inside her would hear them and return a message to guide her.

Those first hours, she was in a trance, not aware of anything or anyone around her. But soon, she realized that she wasn't alone. Scores of people were hiding in the forest, people who looked dirty, swollen and tired, as if they had been beaten. Remembering her father's advice, she made every effort to stay away from them, not taking a path or any direction that looked as if people had been there. She walked through dense vegetation with thick branches hiding her from others but also preventing her from having any idea where she was. She traveled at night, following Sonia's instructions.

Often she felt her way through the forest or imagined a path in her dark travels. The leaves hummed melodies as the wind blew them against each other; she tried to walk to the end of a song, but the songs never ended.

Miriam pushed her way through the forest, trying to imagine herself in a game of hide and seek. In Vilna, she often played a hiding game with her father and brothers. On Polish farms, even small ones, fields of wild grass grew close to the houses, fields that were perfect for hide and seek. Her father and brothers ran from her as she kept her eyes shut and counted to 120. At first she tried jumping above the grass to see them but it was too high. Then she waded through it, hoping to stumble on an unsuspecting brother or her father. At the beginning of the game, her moves were slow, deliberate attempts to catch a hiding person off guard. Then she lost patience, ran one way then another, scurrying frantically in all directions. Always in the end, she fell over a leg and into familiar arms. Miriam hoped it was her brother Jacob's leg because Jacob threw her into the air, high over the grass, allowing quick searching glimpses for the others.

Sometimes it was her father, who hugged her, but then instructed her. "Miriam, you were running around like a crazy person. What good does that do? Listen instead. The wind makes a noise against the blades. Where the noise stops or softens, the blades aren't hitting as much. Perhaps someone is there. Also, you don't have to move all the time. Listen for breathing or for the sound of an arm or a leg moving in the grass."

She would begin slowly, just as her father had instructed. Then she would panic and dart through the grass again. Her worst wounds from this game were scratches on the fingers or lower arm. Jacob kissed her fingers to take away the sting but her father gave her no sympathy.

"Miriam, use your body to push against the grass. It's when you start moving too fast that you use your fingers to push blades away. And don't roll up your sleeves because the grass scratches your bare arms."

He reached over to unroll her sleeves, pulling them back down over her arms. She never told him that she rolled the sleeves up just so he would roll them back down.

Miriam pushed her way through the forest, but when she moved too quickly, no one was there to rescue her. Her legs ached. Strong as she was, Miriam wasn't used to walking endlessly. On long hikes in Vilna, her father said, "Miriam, relax your muscles. Keep them stretched out and you'll enjoy the walk and not have the stress afterwards." She was tense now, but she didn't stop to rest. And still, she refused to follow paths, catching her feet on the roots or trunks of fallen trees. Sometimes, one foot unexpectedly sank into the middle of a trunk, which had disintegrated underneath its bark, and the grubs housed in the decay scurried between her toes.

All the fallen limbs were not of nature's doing. Sometimes, she crossed a section of burnt trees – evidence of German bombers flying over the forest and leaving a souvenir. Often, she thought she was traveling in circles but circles didn't bother her for she had no plan, no direction, and no place to go. Her only goal was to stay away from Germans, and she didn't even know who Germans were. She had never seen one.

Miriam's shoes did not stand up to the rigors of the forest. To make a new pair, she used gifts from nature and lessons from her father. When her feet ached badly, when her handmade shoes of leaves, woven grass and bark no longer protected her from the jagged stone and splintered wood, only then would she give in and travel along a path. Even the path wasn't easy; the pine needles were a constant source of irritation. Those same pine needles that made a comfortable bed also broke her spirit when they stuck in her already scraped and sensitive toes. Mostly, though, she hated the leg pain. It made her think about the time she waded into a cold stream near her farmhouse and hurt herself. She disobeyed her father who trained her since she was a baby to deal with the cold in the late Polish autumns. She walked into the stream to immerse herself in the sound of the water. The streams of Poland rushed down from the mountains through long, narrow, rock tunnels. That rushing sound soothed her so she wasn't aware of the numbness in her feet. The frostbite was bad.

Limping along the path in the forest, she remembered the year she spent on crutches and the sacrifices her family made to ensure her recovery. They all worked together in the fields for twelve and sometimes fourteen hours every day, but after all the work, there was no extra food on the table, no one got new clothes and life seemed to get harder. One expense never got smaller, her doctor bills. Yet the trips to the city for medical care continued, no matter what the financial hardship on the family.

When Miriam struggled along the path in the forest, she wondered if God was punishing her for hurting her family, for walking in cold water when she knew she shouldn't. Miriam hated the leg pain and she hated giving in to it, but mostly she hated the memories – memories of causing her family pain. In the forest, pain and the memories always went together.

Miriam didn't know about the difficulties Jews faced in getting jobs before the War. Her conversations with her parents were not about life's problems. At home, her father didn't talk much, and her mother didn't know what to talk about with her tomboy daughter. Once, her mother said, "I wish you were a boy." Miriam agreed, although she didn't say so to her mother, because she wanted to wear boy's trousers instead of the skirts that always tore on tree limbs.

In the forest now, Miriam remembered her answer to her mother.

"For your sake, Mama, you make me wish I wasn't such a tomboy. But as you always say, it's Papa's fault for letting me tag along after my brothers. He taught them how to skate, run and climb trees and I know he wants me to try the same things. He spends time showing me. You should see how happy he is when I do something right. I like to please Papa."

Miriam wanted her mother to understand.

"When I tie a rope together just like Papa says, and put my feet into it, I climb trees faster than my brothers and it doesn't seem wrong. I like to compete. I can't wait to get outside, Mama. I thought it was Papa I was trying to please, but now I think it's the trees. Did you like trees, water, birds and little animals when you were young?"

Her mother said she preferred the quiet things, the inside things.

Often, Miriam was surprised at her mother's reactions. Miriam liked things that moved and she liked watching things move. She told her mother, "Maybe, I should learn to be gentle and quiet like you. I can tell you see so much. You always watch and then you know. I'm most always running. I like to be moving."

Miriam's mother brushed her hair as they talked and Miriam asked more questions. "Mama, did you like to watch the clouds change shape and imagine new shapes before they formed? I know it's not much use, but is it wrong to wonder with your mind like that?"

Rebecca answered seriously. "It's not wrong. It comes from your father's influence because he loves the out-of-doors so much. Sometimes I think he finds more of God out there than in synagogue."

Then Rebecca hummed a sweet, sad song as she brushed Miriam's hair.

Miriam lost herself in her memories. The trees around her and the trunk upon which she sat were a rest stop. She saw her father gathering wood for the family, and when his arms were full, she joined him for the walk back to the house. Miriam was so intent on the memory that she didn't hear herself singing one of her mother's sad melodies.

When the leg pain disappeared and her feet had power again, she returned to isolated areas. Climbing over rocks and fallen tree trunks took all her energy and concentration, but now she found herself thinking less about where she was and more about how she was going to find food. The wild strawberries finished and the blueberry bushes were drying up. She picked up Vilna nuts, the small round nuts they toasted at home, and now she ate them raw.

When she pitied herself, she would ask the trees over and over, "Why should this happen to me?" until the question became a chant, like her mother's humming. Time passed without clock and without calendar, but she was in the forest for at least three months when she started to sing her question daily. She heard herself and she knew that the tone of her voice had changed. It no longer demanded answers. She didn't know that her body had changed too. She was thin but her arms and legs were swollen, bloated to twice their normal size. Her calves were rounder and wider than her thighs. Her body didn't scare her because it was no more wild than her surroundings. But she guarded her spirit, and it remained constant. She never once admitted to the trees that her loneliness frightened her. If she had said it out loud, her spirit would have escaped in the confession.

In the forest, Miriam was able to find solace in the surroundings. She made friends with the leaves, touching them and patting them, sometimes rubbing her cheeks and arms against them. She took for granted the distant sound of bullets and could almost ignore it. More and more, she followed the music of the leaves. The windier it was, the livelier the music as the leaves sang to each other and to Miriam, soothing her as best they could.

Sometimes, touching the leaves wasn't enough. Hugging the moss covered tree trunks, she fell back against them and imagined the trees were holding her. The moist, soft moss let her sink into the tree, making for a flesh-like embrace.

The more alone she imagined herself, the bigger the tree she sought. She gravitated to the oaks with such full branches and leaves that blackened out almost every speck of sky. She wrapped her arms around their trunks and in turn, the branches and leaves enveloped her. Sometimes, though, her need for human contact was stronger than her fear of people. Then, she forgot what could happen if she were caught, and she left the forest. This day in late autumn, she followed the light at the edge of the forest past a lake and past farmhouses into a town.

It was odd to see life going on normally. People were working their farms, shopping in the town center, and talking to each other. They didn't look evil or menacing, but their innocuous appearance made her fear of capture even more confusing. She thought she might ignore her father's warnings to stay away from people and spend some time in this place.

Miriam didn't realize that the wildness of the forest was now part of her very being. She saw someone point at her and then tell his companion, "Look at that one. Her eyes dart like a bird and she stalks us like a four legged animal." They talked about her with curiosity, not suspicion, for they also saw a harmless child in front of them.

She tilted her head sideways as animals do when they are listening for their prey or for their predators. And her hair was gnarled and gritty. She didn't give up her father's demands for cleanliness but adapted them to her particular needs. Combing hair was not only senseless but troublesome because things got caught in well-kept hair more than in hair left wild. Even more likely, she was conscious of things caught in her hair when she tried to keep it neat so she just stopped combing. What she knew was that she washed her hair every chance she got; she no longer had an inkling of how it looked.

People on this narrow, hard dirt street, avoided her. In adapting to the forest, she guaranteed her isolation and safety from the people who could be her enemies. She had no idea why she shouldn't trust these people, but she recognized fear in their voices and in their eyes, and she knew that people afraid were unpredictable. Because no one talked to her or approached her, she decided this outing was safe. At any rate, her need outweighed her fear. She spent her time watching people, peering at them while pretending indifference at the same time.

She stared at a family walking together. The father was carrying his two children, one on his shoulder and the other in his arms. The mother was following close behind. The man was strong, holding both children with ease and also playing with them as he walked. He leaned one way and then another, tilted one child over his shoulder and tossed the other up over his head. The mother didn't look angry but she wasn't part of the play. Miriam heard the mother tell the father, "You want two roughnecks on your hands? You want your daughter to be a tomboy? So then, enjoy yourself." The man smiled good-naturedly and continued to bounce the children. Miriam found herself drawn to this family and followed them, in step, close behind the mother. This reunion with her memories was a magnet to her loneliness. Even as an outsider, she was still looking at her past, and she was not able to forfeit the feeling of belonging, of having a family.

In the pauses of the couple's conversation, Miriam filled in the words for herself. Her parents always argued over her activities. School in Poland didn't start until children were seven but her father kept her busy during the early years. Once he gave her a rope, showed her how to tie it like a figure eight and put two bare feet inside the loops, using the rest of the rope to brace against a tree as she pulled herself up. Her tree climbing improved but her clothes didn't stand up too well.

When she returned home, her mother voiced her distress, first with Miriam and then with Nathan. Rebecca looked at Miriam, excited and happy after being with her father, and said, "You're a little girl, not a little boy."

Miriam knew better than to answer. Then, Rebecca directed her complaints to Nathan. "You can't treat a girl like a boy. Look at the way she is. She's supposed to be neat and clean like a lady and instead she's a ragamuffin. You've encouraged her to climb trees again. Her legs are scratched and her skirt is dirty from the bark. And her feet are filthy. Do you have to teach her barefoot?"

Rebecca completed her litany of complaints, even though she knew Nathan would continue Miriam's outdoor education. And he responded to her complaints and explained his behavior. "Rebecca, we can't have girls be ladies. We must prepare them for life's challenges. Sometimes, she'll have to be a boy. If you can't understand it, you must find a way to ignore us, to avoid us when we do it."

Miriam knew her behavior was painful for her mother but her father's word was the rule, and she knew her mother would adjust. She worried that one day her mother might wear her father down and then her running and climbing days would stop. Miriam's mother was from the city. She liked good clothes, cleaned and pressed. Nathan was a farmer. He liked the land. While Miriam liked her father's ways, she saw that her mother was somehow smarter. In fact, when the trouble started for Jews in Poland, Rebecca wanted to go to the United States. She was willing to take a chance on something new but Nathan didn't want to leave the land. He saw in it a security and comfort that turned out to be unfounded.

In some ways Rebecca did not give in; Miriam wore dresses even though she always tore them and even though she always begged for pants. Her mother never understood her little girl's attraction to Nathan's lessons. Nathan understood because that is all he knew. To Miriam, the lesson was clear. When she fell, she got up and she survived. In between the falling and the surviving, she was proud of what she did.

Lessons from her mother were the opposite. Miriam's mother spent 20 minutes everyday braiding Miriam's long, thick, blonde hair. Miriam loved the attention but got little satisfaction from this time together, for whenever she came back from outside with her hair in disarray, her mother lectured her about the time it had taken to braid it neatly. As much as she wanted her mother to braid her hair, she learned she paid a price for letting someone else take care of her. Miriam didn't know that her mother would have complained about her daughter's messy hair, no matter who braided it.

"Look what you're doing to her hair," Miriam heard the mother on the street tell her husband after he tossed his daughter up in the air.

Miriam blurred and mingled her past with this family on the road and, now, without realizing it, she was following them into a dry goods shop.

She heard the husband tell his wife that he didn't understand where people got the money to buy clothes now. He pointed to a red silk scarf and told her he would like to see it around her neck. Then, he hugged his children and told them about the coats and toys he would like to buy for them and maybe someday could.

Miriam wanted the man to hug her too, to tell her what he wanted to do for her. In her need, she reached over to put an arm on the only available substitute; a hard, unyielding store mannequin dressed in a soft, gray wool suit with black socks, shoes and tie. She rubbed her fingers over its plaster hair, touched its smooth, plaster cheek, stroked the sleeve of its soft wool arm, and knelt to the floor, wrapping her arms around its hard, unyielding legs.

With her arms around this plastic figure, she thought not of her father but of her mother – her mother's arms around her, taking care of her, braiding her hair. She wanted to be taken care of. Miriam heard her mother's voice, singing softly to her when she was sick.

> *Please my sweet girl, don't cry,*
> *Someday we'll have more food.*
> *Sleep my sweet girl and*
> *You'll forget about your pain.*
> *We had bread in the house*
> *Then the rain came and*
> *We had no more bread.*
> *But we'll have food.*
> *Sleep my little baby, sleep.*
> *Tomorrow is another day.*

But the mannequin was neither father nor mother. She hugged it, but it gave no hug back. And the harder Miriam hugged, the less it gave. She lifted up a trouser cuff to put her hand against its leg and felt only a hard metal rod.

Even with a wetness behind Miriam's eyes, a pressure pushing against her eyes, she did not cry. She pulled the black sock over the metal leg, brushed her fingers against the leather shoe and pulled herself from the mannequin. When she looked up for the father carrying his two children, she couldn't find him.

Miriam walked out of the shop and down the road, retracing her steps. Now she wasn't following anyone. She was taking herself back to the forest.

CHAPTER THREE

December 1941
After being attacked at Pearl Harbor, the
United States enters World War II.

The forest Miriam returned to was a cold one. The pines still had their needles, but the oak trees and the hornbeams had lost their leaves. She wasn't able to hide in the thick darkness and the cold wind blew against her. The wind did not keep her company, as the whispering leaves had, but she wasn't afraid of it. Miriam was about to face the first winter by herself, but the cold didn't worry her. Vilna was cold too and she spent a lot of time outside with her father.

When she was three years old, her father began taking her out in the snow and to swim in a lake. The ritual continued every winter thereafter. He told her that he was preparing her to survive any fate life brought her, but, also, he said, "Cold and snow are no reasons to stay inside. Winters are beautiful. No one should see them from a window." First, they lay in the snow together and then they swam for just a few minutes in the lake. After the swim, Nathan rubbed oil on his body and on Miriam's. Then, they started over again with a swim in the lake and a run through the snow to the oil and a massage. "Going out of water into cold and wet freezes the skin like a burn," he explained. "Oil helps."

Once, he didn't bring oil and showed Miriam another way to protect her skin.

"When your face begins to get hot, as if it's burning, pick up some snow and rub it on your skin. If you do, you won't suffer from frost bite."

When Miriam tried it, the snow stung and she complained to her father.

"That sting is the good part," he told her. "Rub in the snow because it helps your circulation and it makes you almost immune to the cold air. Dry snow is best. Moist snow clings too much. Don't fear the cold. As long as you move around, you'll keep warm enough. Slap yourself and jump up and down.

Winter was also a time for traveling to the steam baths, which were like large hills with fires below and rocks above. Miriam sat with her brothers and her parents on earth benches with wooden planks set over them. The stones were blistering hot from the steam and could never be used as seats. When the stones were hot enough from the open fires, cold spring water was poured over the rocks and then clouds of cleaning, hissing steam rushed up on the sides. On the way to the baths, Rebecca looked for birch trees. She took the smaller branches and tied them into small bundles. Nathan said that a birch massage helped circulation. Rebecca gently hit Miriam's back and body with the branches. Miriam smelled the birch branches as the steam went through them. She knew winter as a wonderful time.

When she needed rest, she searched for the deepest mound of snow and dug a tunnel into it. The snow on top was cold but the layers underneath acted as insulation. No matter how furiously she dug at the tunnel, her fingers still got cold. Then she dug even faster. She knew that as long as she moved, the cold couldn't hurt her. When she finished digging a snow tunnel, she curled up in it and her body gave off enough warmth to heat the space.

"Papa, living outside in winter is not a trip to the lake," she said aloud. He nodded in agreement. "But you can do it. Don't be afraid. Fear will have you make wrong decisions. I know it's hard, but look for the beauty."

She did find the forest beautiful in winter. Icicles hanging from the trees looked like candles and sometimes, when sunlight flickered through the leafless branches, like crystal chandeliers with lit candles burning bright in the dark. Miriam was sure the trees were trying to make her happy.

She tried to imagine the smell of steam and birch but her imagination numbed in these quiet moments. In the quiet moments, she sang herself to sleep with her mother's songs.

Miriam was prepared for the cold of winter, but she had a difficult time finding food in the forest. And, in winter, she shared the forest with wolves who retreated from the mountains in search of food. They couldn't find enough either, and the starving packs roamed the forest, always on a search. The first time she heard their howling, she feared an attack by a pack of wolves more than being captured by German soldiers. Those howls encouraged her departures from the forest, but she would have to leave the safety of the woods anyway – to forage for food at the farms alongside the edge of the forest. Once out of the forest, she searched for train tracks, knowing that trains traveled routes on the outskirts of villages. Then, she waited, waited for a train to appear as a moving silhouette against the glaring white snow. Keeping alert was difficult in the first days out of the forest because the light hurt her eyes, especially the reflected light from the snow.

Trains were her forced companions in the winter. At night, she grabbed on to the side of a slowly moving freight car, pulled herself onto the wooden floor, closed the metal door, and fell asleep to the rocking of the car.

When Miriam slept in a freight car, she found a place in the center of boxes and crates. Even then, she was afraid someone would see her. She never slept well. She preferred to sleep outside and when the wolves didn't scare her, she did.

She left the train in early morning. As soon as she saw a town crossing and, as soon as the cars passed the last few farmhouses, she opened the door just wide enough to slip through. Then, she watched the direction of the train's movement.

"Always jump the way the train goes," she heard her father's instructions each time and then the explanation. "If you jump in the other direction, the wind grabs you and takes you under the tracks." She always remembered what her father said and the wind never pulled her near the cars or the tracks.

On their walks in the countryside, Miriam and Nathan watched the freight trains slow down at village crossings. Miriam begged her father to take a ride with her in one of the boxcars, at least from one village crossing to another. When she was eleven, he relented, but only after explicit instructions about jumping on and off a moving train, no matter how slowly it was moving. They jumped these slow moving freight cars together several times in the next two years, always honoring an unspoken pledge not to tell her mother about their adventures.

When she was desperate for food, she moved toward the farmhouses and sneaked into barns. At dusk, farmers prepared food for the horses and then returned to their houses for dinner. One special offering to the horses was straw pressed thin with molasses to hold it together. Miriam knew about it because she always tried to take it from the horses of her father's friends in Vilna. She sucked the flat, hard straw mixture to get at the sweetness of the molasses.

In these barns, she watched the horses and thought of Lisper, how loyal he was and how much he deserved such a reward at day's end. Otherwise, she resented these horses who looked so fit, so well fed and so cared for. She watched the owners brush their horses for half an hour, wondering if these people who took such good care of their horses knew she was out in the forest uncared for. When a farmer left, she ran into the barn, grabbed a straw molasses cracker and sucked at it furiously. Sometimes, she was so hungry she wanted to chew off pieces, hoping to swallow them and feel something solid go down her throat. But she knew she could lose her teeth that way. Because she only sucked it, one piece lasted for days, and she took great pleasure in tasting the sugar when she was away from the barns and in the forest.

Farmers stored piles of hay in their barns over the winter. Miriam liked sleeping in them more than on the trains. At night, the only movements that first startled her were the scrambling of mice whose winter nests at the bottom of the hay piles were disturbed by her presence. Once she knew what caused the shifting straw, she ignored it. The white, red, and gray mice came to the barn for the same reasons she did. They wanted the warmth of the hay pile and the leftover grain from the horse feedings. If molasses crackers weren't too big for the mice, they would have had them as well.

Once, when Miriam was sure she heard mice, she pushed herself out of the stack to watch them play. But when she did, she saw pairs of black boots shuffling on the ground about twenty feet from the barn doors, which the farmer left open for the first time in a week. Then she saw helmets, round, iron soup bowls covering five heads. The men wore black bands around their sleeves with red and white emblems. She didn't know these patches were the swastika, the symbol of the Nazi party and of the people who were killing Jews.

Miriam dove back into the hay. It shoved into her nostrils, scratching her nose lining and bruising her eyelids and lips with fine, paper-thin splinters and cuts. She dug down until her hands touched empty nests, the mice having scattered when she pushed in. When she was as far under the hay as she could get, she turned her body right side up and pulled it toward the top of the stack. She poked two holes in the straw pile and peered at the soldiers.

German soldiers. They had to be. She couldn't take her eyes from them. They looked strong and confident, not evil as she had supposed they would. The farmer came out to talk to them but she didn't understand the words. The whisperings didn't seem unpleasant and she thought she saw one of the soldiers smile. In the middle of the conversation, one soldier broke the circle and headed toward the barn. She knew she should make a retreat into the hay but she couldn't move. She tried bending her knees and pulling her body down, but every joint froze. She watched the boots get closer and bigger.

Her stillness encouraged the mice to return and one ran over her hand in the trip back to its nest. She pulled her hand away and a section of hay lifted. Sure that the soldier had noticed, she closed her eyes and waited to be grabbed from the pile. When she opened her eyes, she saw the heels of boots walking from the barn door. Perhaps the soldier meant only to stretch his legs.

Miriam stayed in the haystack long into the night. When it seemed as if everyone must be asleep, she left the barn to look for a chicken house, not thinking about taking a chicken but wanting an egg. She carried the egg as she crept into a wheat field, crawling between the rows to a safe place. Miriam cracked it open on the ground and swallowed each half in a gulp. She wondered if she was a thief. She never stole chickens and she didn't kill animals for food but she took some things, just like she took the egg and the molasses crackers.

CHAPTER FOUR

December 1942
Nazi soldiers round up Jews in the city of
Parczew, Poland. Several thousand Jews
manage to escape and reach the dense woods,
thickets and swamps of the nearby forest.
Later, the Nazis hunt down and kill
hundreds of families. Others die of cold,
starvation and disease. Only two hundred
Parczew Jews survive the War in the
Parczew Forest .

A fter a winter in the forest, Miriam was like the wolves who stayed alive but were reduced to near skeletons.

Their eyes and bones seemed to be the only parts of them that didn't shrink. They no longer traveled in packs because the competition for food made them dangerous even to each other. When Miriam saw a lone wolf, his skin hanging loose across his side ribs and his eyes bulging from their sockets, she thought about herself. She didn't know what she looked like, but she recognized herself in the desperation of the wolf.

The second winter she refused to confront the wolves, deciding instead to make her way into one of the villages. Her clothes were no more than rags and, in preparation for the journey, she knew she needed some in better condition. Miriam had seen dead bodies in the forest with clothing, but took them infrequently because she thought that taking someone else's belongings was desecrating the body. Now, in complete desperation, she yearned to share whatever another body could no longer use.

She found the body of a young girl, not much older than herself, who had frozen to death huddled against a big tree, as if she thought the tree would give her warmth. Miriam wondered why the girl didn't known that trees take warmth for themselves. Only snow gives warmth back.

She wrapped herself in the girl's orange scarf of soft wool and in a long brown coat that came from the body of a woman lying close to the girl.

Miriam thought they might have been mother and daughter, but then she wondered why only the woman's body was covered. She thought a mother would have shared the coat. Miriam thought of her mother giving her the coat when she sent Miriam into the forest, the coat left on the cart after Lisper died.

Miriam's fingers searched for a place on this newly found coat to put her parent's wedding ring, the ring she tore from her mother's coat lining before she and Sonia abandoned the cart and most of their possessions. It was hard to find a hiding place on a coat with a hanging hem and with holes where pockets should be.

"Papa, she didn't know to move her fingers in the cold. She pushed them deep into her coat pockets until she wore away the lining. Where shall I keep the ring, papa?"

For the time being, she wrapped it in a piece of hem she tore from the coat and put the small package in her pant's pocket.

Miriam wore the coat and scarf in the hope that villagers would think she was no more than a runaway. The coat hid what was underneath, a thick yellow cotton blouse and boy's short red knee pants. Her feet were bound with thin tree bark softened with a lining of brown oak leaves, moist and pliable in the forest even in the winter. Even though Miriam didn't want to take clothes off the dead in the forest, sometimes, like now, she had to. But she didn't remove shoes. She slipped clothes off bodies but taking shoes meant holding onto someone's foot while she pulled off the shoe. She couldn't wear shoes she took from a dead person.

The snow was heavy this winter. As Miriam walked, it came up over her forest shoes and pressed coldly against her calves. Walking through snow, instead of on top of it, was not a good idea, but she didn't have the patience to build snowshoes. She plodded through a small field, hoping to find a village close by where she could stay until spring.

When she finally saw a larger clearing, it turned out to be fields and more fields of snow. Grayish white clouds hung in oblong patterns from the blue and gray toned sky over this white floor. The open fields would be her path, even though she knew similar fields were the death walk for Lisper and Sonia. She could not return to the forest where only the starving wolves were waiting for her.

Miriam didn't understand the weather and its connection to the war, anymore than she understood the war itself. If the weather was pleasant, the forest was good to her and food was everywhere. If it rained too much, fruits rotted, and if it was too cold, plants died.

She wished for pleasant, dry weather while everyone else in Poland was grateful for heavy rain in the spring and harsh cold in the winter. If the usual rains had come in the spring when the Germans invaded Poland, the forests would have flooded and the marshes would have been impossible to pass with troops. The mild weather, which made it tolerable for her the first months in the forest, condemned Poland to a pathetic defeat by the German army.

Miriam didn't know she had little to fear in crossing these snow packed fields. Harsh weather stopped German reconnaissance, and the threat of more snow, suspended in the hanging clouds, was almost a guarantee that German soldiers wouldn't make a surprise appearance.

When she walked through the fields, the snow reached her knees and soaked through her ragged coat, hanging on like it would to a tree branch. Snow seeped through her braided, bark shoes and stuck between the leaves that coated her feet from the bark. Instead of soft protection, these leaves were becoming a menace. Taking away the leaves meant dealing with cuts and bruises from bark rubbing against her feet, but the wet and snow covered leaves were too heavy and, now, she could barely drag herself forward.

Slipping out of one shoe and bending over to unwrap the leaf binding, she lost her balance and fell face first into the snow. She didn't have the power to get up and when she moved, she sank further into the snow. She thrashed her hands and feet, splattering snow everywhere. She started to yell, "Papa, Papa!" but snow filled the inside of her mouth and when she tried to spit it out, more packed itself in. Her teeth and gums were like one ice mass that would crack with the slightest touch.

Just as the cold exploded in her head, she heard echoes of "Don't panic, Miriam. Don't panic." Her father was talking to her and she heard him. Her body relaxed. First, her legs bent slowly at the knees and shifted her body forward. Then her waist, chest and shoulders pulled upwards and finally, her neck and head lifted slowly. A twist of her neck sent snow off her head but she had to pull the snow out of her mouth, wiping her fingers against her gums to get rid of the cold moisture sticking to her tongue and mouth lining.

She unwrapped the orange scarf, removed the coat and jumped up and down, slapping her hands against her body. She reached around as far as she could to hit her back and shoulders, but her arms weren't long enough to do much good. Her father had always rubbed her back for her and she wanted him now.

"Papa, I'm doing as you said," she whispered, waiting for a warm hand across her back. When it didn't come, she rubbed her coat with the scarf, shook out the scarf, put both back on and continued across the field. She walked for hours and was so much into the habit of expecting no view that she was past two farmhouses before she realized she was entering a village.

She walked toward buildings, more than she saw together anywhere in a small town. If she hadn't been so determined to leave the forest, she would have feared the numbers. Now she looked forward to mixing, perhaps unnoticed, in the center of this village.

The overcast sky was a weather forecast. Already, snow started to fall lightly but anyone who watched the clouds knew another storm was close by. Townspeople were lined up in front of the stores. Miriam didn't know it but most villagers had used up their winter supplies, and this new bout with the weather was unexpected. People were anxious to buy whatever food they could with the little money they had.

Shoppers were talking to each other about how happy they were that winter kept the Germans away. Those closest to shop windows were examining the products inside. Miriam stopped to look with them.

At the butcher shop, she saw chopped beef shaped into large molds, chickens and smoked pork swinging from the window top, stew-meat soaked in onions and garlic piled high on top of each other, and herring marinated or creamed in barrels along the window.

She didn't move from the window, and the conversations, repeated with each new group that passed by, were meaningless to her. Two women complained to each other.

"We won't have any meat at all soon."

"Look, there's hardly any in the window and it's only late morning. The butcher says they take more meat than they let him sell. If his prices are high, he doesn't want the blame. Each week, he says he doesn't know if he'll be in business the next."

"He's been coming to the farms, hoping to butcher directly for the farmers, but they found out about it and are asking for supplies from the farmers as well."

"I buy what I can and hope it will last."

Miriam didn't know Nazi soldiers took food from the merchants. Nor did she know that local collaborators told on people who tried to hide any of their merchandise.

Miriam turned to look at the women, trying to discover how such misery could come from so much food. The women looked full, maybe even fat, although she couldn't tell because their bodies were covered in thick, black fur coats. Their matching fur hats covered everything but their round faces, and their boots came up well under their coats.

The boots tempted Miriam to look away from the trays of meat. Her feet were cut everywhere and only the cold was keeping them from bleeding. It was hard to decide what she wanted more, their boots or the food. At least the food was possible. She wanted to go in and grab a piece, at least of the herring, and swallow it before they caught her. But the idea of taking anything from the store scared her. She heard they cut off people's fingers for stealing. In the forest, she tried not to steal but sometimes her survival depended upon it. If she were to make a new life outside the forest, no one would have taught her what to do. Perhaps she would have to steal. But if she had no fingers, she couldn't take a thing.

She wandered up and down the street, stopping at each window displaying food. The bakery window showed loaves of dark pumpernickel, rye crusted with corn meal, and puffed white egg bread all in twists like the challah she had at home on Friday nights. Although the window was piled high, she saw that inside the shelves were empty. This bakery had no pastry, no rolled dough filled with prunes and raisins, the smell of which could change freezing winter air into a warm, Shabbat, Friday night, kitchen.

The grocery store wasn't made for window-shopping. Windows were small, and the line of people waiting to get in was so big that it covered the view. Woman after woman held empty sacks crocheted of twine and meant to expand to many times their unfilled size.

Miriam stood across the way from the line, watching people leave the store. Sacks were still limp as people left. She imagined herself packing such a bag so full that the twine would make ridges against the food, food to last more than one winter in the forest.

As she imagined herself with such a package, she made her way into the line toward the small market, her hand limp at her side but her fingers clutching at imaginary thick rope handles of a bag.

She continued forward as the line moved, always holding her hand down, as if raising it would somehow allow the bag to disappear. A woman behind her brought her son and daughter into town but they were getting bored with the long wait. They poked and pulled at each other but they were bored with that too now. Then they saw Miriam. At first, the girl made faces at her. But making faces wasn't enough for the boy. He started pulling at her scarf and stepping on her feet. When Miriam didn't respond, the boy, no more than ten, shouted, "Mother, it's a girl animal in front of us." Then, he grabbed Miriam's orange scarf and pulled it off.

Miriam yanked up her hand, clutching both arms tightly to her chest to protect the bag she was sure he was going to take from her. The mother must have thought Miriam was going to hit her son because she stepped in between the two. But when she looked down, all she saw was a frightened girl grabbing on to a torn brown coat. Miriam's eyes were darting everywhere at once. Her hair was sticking out in all directions, almost as if it was frozen that way. Her bark shoes, now more dried out, had warped on her feet.

The woman's hand rested on Miriam's shoulder, maybe as an apology for her son or maybe as a warning for Miriam not to do anything to retaliate. While the woman's hand was on Miriam's shoulder, Miriam leaned in her direction.

"Mama, Mama, she's a crazy one," the boy shouted. Then he danced around Miriam, hopping and jumping to his own chants. The woman ignored her son and Miriam. He stopped teasing when he realized Miriam would not respond and began to fight again with his sister.

The line moved forward and Miriam followed as if being pulled slowly and methodically by a long rope. At the door, she stopped and the woman, as if she expected it, moved around her. Miriam stayed at the front door, close enough to smell the onions and garlic hanging from the ceiling on long ropes. Even the flour had a special odor and its powder, invisible before, now filled the store with a white cloud so thick she was sure she could bite into it if only she could get into the store.

She was in the same spot when the woman and her two children left the store. The boy was carrying a bag, the weight of which he easily managed with one hand, while he slapped at Miriam's orange scarf with the other. "Look, the crazy one is still here."

Then the girl noticed Miriam or at least she watched her brother go after the scarf as a boy would pull at a dog's tail for no reason other than it was there. For perhaps no more reason than her brother, she said to her mother. "Let's take her with us," as if she wanted a stray dog to have a home.

The mother bent over Miriam – examining her hair, her eyes, her coat and even her bark shoes. Miriam stood still, head down, but her hands clutched ever harder at the bag against her chest. The woman straightened up.

"You can come with us," she said.

She reached for Miriam's hand and her daughter reached for the other one. Miriam's eyes darted down, watching for the bag to fall to the ground. Nothing fell. She was pulled along the road and she didn't fight, not even when the boy slapped at her.

CHAPTER FIVE

August, 1943
The deportation of 40,000 Jews from the
Bialystok ghetto to Treblinka precipitates
two major revolts. After the Bialystok
rebellion, more than 1,000 Jewish children
are seized in the city and deported.

Minutes after their arrival to the family's
house, the woman told Miriam to undress,
but Miriam stood, not moving, while the
mother and daughter prepared a tub of hot water. They
pushed Miriam in front of it and again told her to undress, but
it was as if Miriam were deaf. She did not respond. The
daughter tugged at the brown coat sleeves while the mother
lifted Miriam's arms. Miriam allowed herself to be undressed,
like a mannequin. When the coat was off, her hands dropped
back to her sides.

The girl unbuttoned the yellow blouse and although
Miriam stiffened when she put her hand on the blouse, she
didn't move away. The mother pulled down the red knee
pants and Miriam was naked in the room, except for her bark
shoes. Slowly, she stepped out of them.

The brother watched from his chair in the dining area.
When Miriam was nude, he jumped from his place, wrapped
his arms around her waist and clenched his hands together.

57

"Look, she's a little nothing," he said. He put one hand on her abdomen. "She's got no stomach." Then he flattened the other hand against her chest. "Mama, she doesn't even have a bump here."

The sister tried to push him away but he grabbed on to Miriam's thigh and slapped her buttocks. "She's got no bottom either. She's a girl cause I don't see no peter but she sure is missing something."

Miriam didn't move an arm in protest of his molesting or even shift her body to skirt his advances. Once, though, she looked at the sister, who didn't notice the plea for help.

The mother continued preparing Miriam for the bath as if her son were not there and when she guided Miriam to the tub, the son left to take his viewing position from the dining area chair.

The woman told her daughter to lift Miriam's feet one at a time and place them in the tub. Then, she put her hands on Miriam's shoulders and pushed her into a sitting position in the water.

For two years, Miriam's baths were in cold lakes. The heat of this water penetrated her skin as if she were scalded from the inside. She tried to straighten a leg but the metal edge of the tub burnt the sole of her foot and she pulled back with a jerk that sent water splashing over the girl and her mother.

The girl talked to Miriam for the first time. "Don't touch the tub, the metal gets really hot. You'll get blisters if you're not careful and they hurt for a long time. We put a lot of kettle water in the bath to get you clean."

Miriam pulled her legs up until her knees touched her chest and was drawing her arms toward her body when the woman leaned over, put her hands on Miriam's shoulders and shoved as hard as she could. Miriam's head went under, the hot water forcing itself into her mouth and burning the inside of her cheeks and under her tongue. Even her nose lining was burning as if someone poured boiling water from a teakettle down her nostrils.

The woman held her under until she was satisfied that every strand of Miriam's hair was soaked. Then she reached under Miriam's chin and lifted her head from the water. She rubbed the homemade bar of soap over her back, legs, stomach and chest with a pressure that brought pain to every part she touched.

This bath could not have been any different from the steam baths and the mild birch branch thrashings in Vilna but the woman did it without love or care. The same force and heat caused discomfort instead of pleasure, and Miriam's body was no longer used to these conditions.

The woman shoved her under the water again, but in preparation, Miriam tightened her lips and blew air out her nose. The efforts were unnecessary because the woman only wanted to get the soap rinsed off and she stopped when Miriam's shoulders went under. Then she rubbed the bar of soap into Miriam's head, not noticing that Miriam's long hair was falling over her face. The soap dripped into her eyes. The son walked over to the tub, grabbed a handful of wet hair and pulled. Miriam's eyes started to pour tears and for the first time, the mother slapped her son's hand and grabbed it off Miriam's hair.

Before the mother could stop him, he took his other hand, collected the rest of the hair hanging down from Miriam's back, and threw it over her face. She tried to push the hair away, and the soapsuds with it, but she only succeeded in rubbing the soap in her eyes. Trying to help, the mother shoved her under the water to rinse her hair and get the soap off her face. Only again she took Miriam by surprise and the sudsy water filled her mouth and went through her nose as she inhaled. The worst was that her eyes were open and the dirty water bathed them in the suds.

This time, she pushed her head out of the water. Her eyes were fighting their own battle and liquid was streaming out of them. Her shoulders started to shake and her head began bobbing up and down. She couldn't control herself. Except for her first hours alone in the forest, Miriam didn't cry. Now, she couldn't stop.

Water from the tub splattered across the wooden floor and both the mother and the daughter moved back. Even the son, who came over to watch, stayed away from the tub. It looked as if an animal had discovered a small watering hole in the middle of summer. Miriam slapped her hands at her side, her shoulders hitting the back part of the oval tub and her feet pushing against the metal sides.

She was frantically gulping for air. Strained, rasping noises were coming from the back of her throat. Then the inhaled air exploded through her nose like a sneeze, only the mucous that streamed out softened the sounds so that they sounded more like weeping than sneezing.

Just as the outburst began without warning, it stopped. The sounds didn't fade; they just ceased. The movement didn't slow; Miriam just froze. After a few seconds, Miriam lifted her hand and rubbed the back of it across her nostrils, wiping away the mucous.

The son moved toward the tub and pointed his hand at the water. "Now there's boogers in the thing. She's got the bath water full of boogers."

He rubbed his hand across one of her shoulders. "I even feel'em. She's got a slime on her. I'm not cleaning out that tub this time. Nobody's gonna make me."

His sister shoved him from the tub area, knocking him onto the stone hearth of the fireplace.

"You pee in the tub and that's worse. You leave her alone or I'll beat your rear, you know I will too."

The boy cowered against the hearth but then he walked over to the tub and spit in the water. His sister smacked him so fast that she hit a cheek still puffed out from the act of collecting saliva. He tried to slap her back but she caught his hand before it started a forward motion.

"Wlodek, I'm telling you to leave her alone. You'll pay if you don't, cause I'll swat you all over the place. You can peeve me and get away with it, momma always lets you. But you keep pestering now and you're gonna produce plenty of your own boogers."

Wlodek backed away. His sister reached over to pull a towel hanging by the fireplace. Miriam shaped the name Wlodek with her lips but no one saw and she made no sound to match.

"Now stand up," the girl directed Miriam. "It's really cold, so you've got to dry fast."

Miriam moved only when the girl placed her hands under Miriam's armpits and lifted. The girl rubbed Miriam's body rapidly, drying her off quickly. Miriam said quietly, "My father would want me to roll in the snow first."

The girl lifted her head, waiting for more conversation but Miriam didn't say anything else so she introduced herself, "My name is Erenka and I'm 14 years old."

She expected an answer but nothing came. Although when she was drying Miriam's other leg, Miriam tried to pronounce Erenka, again shaping the sound but not saying it out loud.

The mother brought some of Erenka's clothes and they dressed Miriam in a long sleeve, coarse cotton shirt and a long wool skirt frayed at the hem where it looked as if someone had worn the skirt too long, stepping on the hem as she walked. The socks were handmade but thin and loosely knitted cotton, not the tight, wool knee-highs Miriam wore in Vilna.

Erenka looked at the long skirt on Miriam and explained, "I always make my mother let me have long skirts because my feet are always cold. Then, I walk over the hems and she complains that I ruin my skirts. You have on one of my skirts that she made last winter."

Miriam nodded her head.

"You're so clean now," Erenka said, "but the bath water wasn't dirty like we thought it would be. You looked like you'd be dirty but you weren't. Where did you come from?"

"Where am I?" Miriam answered back.

"You're in Luba. Why don't you know where you are?"

Miriam didn't answer any questions but the girl kept asking anyway. "I'd like to know your name."

That one Miriam answered. "Pesla, my name is Pesla."

For the first time in two years, someone wanted to know who she was. Miriam answered out of her own need more than to satisfy the girl's curiosity, but she knew to give a Polish name, not her Jewish one.

"The girl's name is Pesla," Enreka shouted to her mother. "She told me her name."

Her mother didn't answer, but Wlodek shot back, still from the corner of the fireplace, "It's an ugly name. Pesla is an ugly name."

Erenka wanted to know all sorts of things about Miriam. She asked questions nonstop, ignoring the fact that Miriam didn't answer. Instead, she answered herself.

"How old are you? I told you I was 14."

"What kind of school do you go to? I used to go to a one room school but now we have five different subjects in a big building and some of my teachers are German."

"Do you know German? I had to learn. At school they make you."

"Where are your parents? My father is in the war. He's not a soldier but the Germans tell him what to do."

"She's not answering your questions," Wlodek said to annoy his sister. "Stop replyin' to your own questions." Then he stepped in front of Miriam and she backed away from him this time, remembering his pleasure in yanking her hair.

"My father's out looking for Jews, Pesla," he said. "You're lucky you got yellow hair. If you had brown, I'd know you was a Jew. We wouldn't take in a Jew, would we Mother? We'd bring her to the center of town where we got her and give her to the German soldiers. Course they wouldn't take Pesla. Naked, she's like a stick."

Miriam was tired of Wlodek but he no longer frightened her. He stopped touching her and she didn't think anyone in the family would turn her in, but she didn't understand why he was so mean. She didn't know how or why but Germans had made people hate Jews. She didn't know who these Germans were. How did they know her? For the last two years, she stayed away from people because her father had told her that she should. Now she understood that she wouldn't be safe anywhere but in the forest. Even if Erenka and her mother would keep her, she would have to lie about not being Jewish. She wouldn't say anything to this family to let them know she was Jewish. The Russians should have taken Wlodek, she thought, not her brother Jacob. Wlodek needed to be punished, not her, not Jews. Miriam didn't stop to think that Wlodek was not even ten and her brother had been a young man when the Russians took him. For Miriam, Wlodek was not a child but a formidable, although no longer feared, opponent.

The mother set the table and the smells from the grocery filled the room, only now the vapors from the simmering pot mingled with the air of the room.

Miriam inhaled the meal through her nose – cabbage borscht and beef with garlic and pepper – long before she tasted it. They sat around the table, each place set with a large spoon and a bowl. Every person had a glass for the homemade jug of wine in the center of the table.

As the mother ladled out the soup, she spoke to Miriam. "I am Lica Dobovsky. I took you in because my daughter wanted it. The life of a gypsy child can't be a good one, especially now. You're welcome to stay here as long as you like and I'll try to treat you fairly. Of course you'll have work to do, but even the children have chores and yours won't be much harder. We don't have a lot of food but so far we've always had enough and neither my husband or I have been ones to watch children starve in the winter."

Mrs. Dobovsky finished pouring the soup and looked at Miriam as she talked but Miriam bent her head toward the table. She didn't realize the woman had finished.

"Pesla, do you have anything to say?" Lica Dobovsky reached over to put her hand under Miriam's chin, lifting her head.

"Thank you."

"Eat your borscht, Pesla, or it will get cold."

Wlodek and Erenka scooped up the cabbage from the soup and were lifting the bowls to drink the juice before Miriam had taken her first spoonful. They watched her eat. She sucked in the cabbage, and it went down her throat before she had a chance to bite into it. A piece got caught and she coughed it up.

"Pesla, you just swallowed that piece whole," Erenka said. "Where have you come from? Who taught you to eat like that?"

Miriam didn't answer but after that she chewed each piece of cabbage until it was small, soft shreds on the back of her tongue. Only then, she gulped inward, letting the cabbage slip down her throat. She was full after the third spoonful but her bowl showed hardly anything had been eaten. She pushed the cabbage into her mouth until the bowl contained only the greenish yellow liquid, the cabbage broth spiced with salt, pepper and garlic.

Just as her mother had taught her, she dipped the spoon in the bowl and lifted it to her mouth, not even bending to meet the spoon. She was looking down when Wlodek and Erenka drank their soup from the bowl. If she had seen, she

65

would have been clever enough to do the same. Now, they had another chance to question her.

"You don't look like no lady, so you don't have to act like one," Wlodek said. "You sure got funny habits for a gypsy girl. Are you sure you're not a Jew? Answer me, why don't you? You can talk, I heard you before with my sister."

"Wlodek, you have to leave her alone," Erenka said. "She'll never talk to any of us if you don't let up and we'll never know where she came from."

Then, turning to Miriam, "You want us to know about you, don't you? Just tell us a little something."

Miriam picked up the bowl and began drinking the soup, hoping her behavior would be enough to satisfy them. But now Erenka was as openly curious as her brother was mean. She wanted to know about Miriam's family.

"Pesla, how could your parents let you leave them? Do you have a mother and a father? Where are they?"

"I don't know for sure where they are," Miriam answered, not lying. "They don't know where I am either."

"How long have you been traveling by yourself? How can you take care of yourself? I wouldn't know what to do if I were separated from my parents. Don't you need someone?"

Miriam lifted the bowl to her mouth again and drank until the soup was gone. Having no other excuse to hold the bowl to her lips, she set it down but she didn't answer Erenka. Miriam was afraid to tell her that she'd been living in the forest. Surely, the family would know that she was hiding because she was Jewish.

"I want you to answer me, Pesla."

"I can't," Miriam answered.

When Miriam's empty bowl touched the table, Madame Dobovsky placed in it four bite size pieces of beef, stewed in garlic juice.

"I wish I had more to give you because I can see you haven't eaten well for a long time but meat is scarce, especially in the winter. Often the German soldiers come first and we're lucky if we get chicken."

Miriam picked up a piece of meat with her fingers. She had watched Wlodek and Erenka, and pushed it into her mouth as they did. Miriam didn't want to choke again so she chewed until her jaws hurt, but the meat didn't break up. The nuts in the forest were easier to eat than this meat. Even her teeth were getting sore against her gums. Finally, she swallowed and put a second piece in her mouth.

She wanted to stop eating. Her stomach was bloating and her intestines were turning in every direction. She remembered her father's advice. "Even after one day of fasting on Yom Kippur, Miriam, you must ease into foods the next day. One day of not eating and your stomach has adjusted to less. If you eat a heavy meal to break the fast, you'll get sick."

"Papa, I have to eat this food. I need to stay somewhere."

"What did you say, Pesla? You mumble so much that neither my mother nor I can hear you."

"I'm full," she said to Erenka.

"You can't be. You've only had a small piece of meat. Please, eat more."

""I don't want her to eat no more. I'll take it. It should have been mine anyhow." Wlodek stuck his fingers into

Miriam's bowl, pulled the beef across her face and stuck it into his mouth. "Now we're both happy."

Erenka began to protest but stopped. Across the table, Miriam was bent over the side of her chair, throwing up. Madame Dobovsky reached over to touch her shoulder but Miriam shook off her hand. Between spasms, she managed to say out loud, "I meant to listen Papa, I did."

"Pesla, do you want something? We can't understand you. Just tell us what you need. My daughter and I will try to help."

Miriam threw up once more and then her stomach stopped heaving. The tightness left her abdomen and her body uncurled itself. She picked up the spoon and bowl from the table, kneeled on the floor and began to scoop the vomit. Lica Dobovsky brought large cotton rags to the floor and cleaned up the mess before Miriam even filled the bowl. Then she took a damp rag to Miriam's mouth.

"You had too much of a day. You need a long night. After some sleep, you'll be fine. Erenka, get a nightgown."

Erenka and her mother undressed Miriam as they had done earlier for the bath. Nude again, she made a ready target for Wlodek. He came from behind and grabbed his hands together against her stomach. "You got anything left to throw up in that little round nothing?"

Her sore stomach couldn't handle the pressure and she doubled over in pain, pulling Wlodek with her. He thought Miriam had thrown him on purpose and he retaliated. While she was bent over, he grabbed her buttocks with one hand and goosed her with two fingers from the other hand.

Miriam's body jerked but she made no other protest. The mother saw what he was doing but he moved to fast for her to stop him. Now, she smacked the back of her hand across his cheek with enough force to throw him a few feet away.

"Wlodek, you get worse every day your father is away. I don't know what to do with you anymore. If you don't leave Pesla alone, you'll find yourself without a few meals. Maybe then you'll see what it's like to need food. Now stop picking on Pesla."

"Pesla is a yellow haired Jew, I know it. She's the reason my father is away. I don't want her here."

"She'll stay here because she has no place else to go," Madame Dobovsky answered.

Miriam stood naked during this exchange until Erenka slipped a nightgown over her head. She listened intently to the mother and wanted to believe what she said.

Madame Dobovsky, considering the incident over, addressed the sleeping arrangements. "Pesla, you share the side of the room with Erenka and Wlodek won't bother you. You wake me up if he does."

She led Miriam to a down mattress on the floor, covered her with two wool blankets, and left the room.

Miriam was sleeping inside a house. No wind, no snow, no wolves, no boxcars, and no haystacks. If she missed the forest, her body didn't know it. The comfort of the house lulled her to sleep.

Miriam woke when it was still dark and cold but she saw the outline of Wlodek's body, also on the floor, covered in blankets and hugging the wall for more warmth. Her eyes adjusted more easily to dark than light, because it was always dark in the forest. Quickly, she searched the room for Erenka, finding her on a bed with only her face showing under the layers of covers.

Satisfied that both were asleep, Miriam slid out from under the blankets. During her bath, she watched where they put her clothes and she went directly to the small table by the fireplace. The clothes weren't there but her shoes were still under the table. While she was stepping into them, she saw her clothes in a bundle on the floor close by. Miriam was glad that they hadn't been thrown away. She wanted to leave with the clothes she found in the forest not a skirt of Erenka's and surely not any pants of Wlodek's. She pulled the nightgown over her head, put on the red knee pants, and slipped her arms into the sleeveless yellow shirt. The brown coat lay beneath her clothes and she bent to pick it up. Her stomach still hurt at the move.

Without even a glance around the room, she walked toward the door and into the winter morning.

"Papa, they ask too many questions. I couldn't stay," she said out loud.

When her warm body hit the cold air, her stomach got nauseous again. She walked no more than ten steps when she began to throw up. She picked up some snow, put it into her mouth and then spit it out. She rubbed fresh snow around her lips and walked toward the forest in the direction she remembered. The dark welcomed her.

CHAPTER SIX

September 1943
Nazis attempt to round up all 7,500 Danish
Jews. They fail. The Danes not only
warn the Jews but also help them escape
to neutral Sweden.

With each step toward the forest and away from the family, Miriam's body relaxed more. The forest was her haven, but her need for family was stronger than she was willing to admit. Just a short time after leaving the Dobovsky family, on one early evening , she came upon a clearing. She didn't ask herself whether it was by will or by accident. The clearing was there and across it, five houses, with light coming from each. The yearning to be with her parents grew stronger the longer she hid in the forest, and she ran toward the middle house as if she were going home, as if the years in the forest were no more than a lonely dream.

The cold, wet ground slowed her. Otherwise, she might have burst through the door. Instead, she stopped a few yards from the house. The mud plastered to her feet was so heavy that she couldn't move another step. Scraping the cold muck from her bark shoes with bare fingers was enough to remind her that she wasn't in Vilna, that she dare not enter this house. She thought about the Dobovsky family and

71

actually turned to go back to the forest, but her legs would not take her; she could not make them. Instead, they began toward the house, walking sideways, as if belonging to someone intoxicated.

Through a window, Miriam watched the fire light up the room. She guessed the time of day by the fire, certainly in its beginning stages for the evening. The people were about to have dinner, she thought, because they were sitting around the table. Dusk was a dangerous time to be near households, for the evening chores might not be complete and a trip to the barn was a good possibility. Miriam was cautious. She watched the farmer carefully, promising herself she would hide immediately if he moved toward the door.

Miriam stared as this farm family sat at the table with soup bowls in front of them. She remembered the sour leaf soup her mother had ready for them when they came back from a day of collecting firewood. The meal was always ready, but first they took off their shoes and walked across the papered floor to the dining table. Their fingers were still red from the cold and from the icy water they used to wash outside the house. The well froze early in the cold weather so even though her brothers worked all day, they went to the lake to chop through perhaps a meter of ice to get a few buckets of water for drinking, cooking and washing.

Miriam would wrap her hands around a bowl of hot shav – sour leaf, borscht – and then pull away at the burning touch. "Miriam, heat doesn't always make warmth," her father said when he saw her pull back. He told her that movement provided warmth, often better than heat, which plays funny tricks on the body. The soup bowl wasn't hot enough to burn her, but her hands were so cold that the skin couldn't adjust to the temperature difference. If she let her hands warm up naturally, bent her fingers and twisted her wrists, and then touched the soup bowl, she got pleasure instead of pain.

As Miriam watched the family inside this farmhouse, she moved her fingers up and down in slow, even patterns.

The family inside was finishing the meal and the woman was collecting bowls from the table. Miriam thought about her mother clearing the table and then bringing over the samovar. Rebecca gathered small chips of wood, burned down to small coals in the brick oven. Then, she opened the bottom of the samovar and slip the glowing wood chips inside. She placed a handful of tea leaves in the angular metal urn and poured in the water. While the tea was brewing and then for as long as the children wanted, each told about the day. When everyone finished drinking the tea, Rebecca closed the special lid over the samovar, which stopped the air from circulating through the wood coals underneath. When the container cooled, she removed the chips, keeping them for the next evening.

Rebecca also used small wooden coals to heat her iron and she saved this chore for after dinner. The iron had an opening in the bottom about an inch thick for coals and a special cover between the air holes on the bottom and the chip container, so that the ashes wouldn't fall on the clothes.

Outside this strange farmhouse, Miriam heard her mother complaining while she ironed. "Miriam, I hope you see how nice this skirt looks now and how long it takes to get it that way. Tomorrow, you'll be climbing trees in it and nobody knows what else. I don't recognize you as the same child in morning and at night."

"Mama, don't iron the skirt," Miriam answered. "Then you won't be disappointed in me. I feel good wrinkled. When you dress me in the morning, I want to take the bottom of the skirt between my hands and twist as hard as I can. I watch you in the evening, seeing how much care you take with my clothes and I feel bad. Don't iron my clothes."

"You'll start the day like a lady. How you finish is not in my control."

Rebecca stopped her ironing to brush her hand against Miriam's cheek and kiss her forehead. Her mother's hand was warm from the heat of the iron.

Outside this farmhouse, Miriam rubbed her fingertips across her cheek. Her fingers were cold and gave no comfort to her cheek.

Two children got up from the table, walked over to the fireplace and sat in front of it. Miriam noticed their shoes crossing the natural wood floor. Her mother made her take off her shoes at the door, having her walk around in heavy wool stockings. The decision wasn't for Miriam's comfort but for the appearance of the house. Rebecca's wooden floors were clean, so clean that few people actually saw them because she insisted on covering them with newspaper. As long as it was wet outside, the Kornitsky's floors were covered with paper.

Miriam lapsed back and forth from watching the family inside the farmhouse to memories of her Vilna farmhouse. As she watched these farmhouse children get ready for bed, she thought of herself and her brothers. She watched these children unroll their mattress and knew they would be sleeping together. Miriam's house in Vilna had two big rooms and the children could sleep anywhere they placed the mattresses that night. Her three brothers shared one gigantic mattress filled with straw, flat and big enough for all three of them. She had one small mattress to herself although, when she was a young girl, she often begged to sleep with her brothers.

Miriam watched these children getting ready for bed and yearned to sleep on the mattress with them. She needed to make them her family. The mother was in a rocking chair in front of the fire and her lips were moving. Miriam thought she could hear her and mouthed the words to a sad Russian folk song.

> *The sky is huge with many clouds,*
> *No sound disturbs the quiet night.*
> *The rifts between the clouds are filled*
> *With stars conversing at their height.*
> *The sky grows dark and overcast.*
> *I seek to walk a different way*
> *Where loving arms will lift me close*
> *And guide a child who's gone astray.*
> *I walk, I run, I don't escape*
> *For somehow, sorrows follow me.*
> *But sleep's caress lets me forget,*
> *Lets me pretend in dreams I'm free.*

Without being aware, Miriam sang the song aloud, soothing herself with her voice. The words were hers but the melody was her mother's.

> *The clouds around me are deep.*
> *I can't see anything.*
> *When will God give me the sunshine*
> *So I can see not by touch or by feel.*
> *Oh, God, how long can I run like this,*

Without clothes, without food, without shoes.
Don't you love me?
I have nobody to talk to but the
Stars and the trees.
I wish the time would come
When my mother would pick me up
Like a baby and sing me a song

Now, she was in her mother's sad world, lost in the songs and melodies of despair. She rocked herself back and forth, oblivious to the family inside or to her surroundings. She didn't see the husband bend over his wife, whisper something to her, and reach for his coat. She didn't see him open the door. She wasn't aware that he saw her when he went outside. He walked toward Miriam and, still, she continued singing and swaying. When he put his hand on her shoulder, she leaned into it. Then her body steeled. She turned toward him because his arm was pulling her that way, and for an instant, she met his eyes. He was framed against the window, his face not clear because it was backlit from the firelight remaining in the room. She could see him searching her face.

Miriam pulled away and ran, not saying anything to him and not knowing what he would do. He didn't follow, but she didn't look back to see either.

The clearing, which had been such a short walk in the early evening, was an obstacle course now. She tripped over roots and caught her feet in small holes. The impact from running so hard forced her feet into the cold, soggy ground and they picked up heavy clumps of mud, so that by the time she reached the forest, she was like a movie running in slow motion.

The ground was cold, the wet dirt stuck to her clothes and her feet were covered with mud to the ankles. Yet the heaviest weight came from inside. She laid her face against a tree trunk and whispered to it, "I have no family."

CHAPTER SEVEN

June 1944
Allied forces land on the beaches of
Normandy. No relief or rescue operations
are undertaken for concentration camp
victims. The position of the Allies is that
relief and rescue can be achieved only by a
military victory over the Nazis.

Miriam heard her father's voice less often. Everything she did in the forest was the same. Everyday was the same. For weeks, months and now years, she walked in the forest in the night and she slept anywhere she could, in any cave she could find, during the day. She had no pleasure from surviving another winter. Spring was no better. She was not as careful anymore, and her legs were scratched badly from the edges of broken branches and jagged rocks. Sometimes, even brushing against leaves caused thin scrapes on her arms and legs.

An infection, even a small one, could kill her. Miriam knew the danger of these injuries. Her father told her many times that a simple open sore left unattended could easily get infected. "Sometimes," he said, "People die from these infections because they spread throughout the body." Cleanliness was one way to avoid infection. Trying not to get cut or scrapped was another. Because Miriam was injuring her feet all the time now, cleanliness was not enough to heal the sores. She needed stronger remedies. She used potatoes, even though getting the potatoes meant leaving the forest and digging in farmers' fields.

In Vilna, when Miriam was five, she tripped over fallen branches and cut her forehead on some rocks. Even though the cuts were minor, blood was all over her face and clothes. Crying and hysterical, she ran home. Her father was more concerned with her hysterics than with the injuries. "Miriam, why are you so afraid? The cuts on your forehead are small ones. The layer of skin is thin there and blood flows close to the surface so any little cut bleeds a lot. If you see blood, don't be afraid. There are such simple ways to stop it."

He led her into the kitchen, took a potato, sliced it in half and grated it to a rough pulp. Then, he scooped up a handful of the grated potato and pressed it against her forehead. Nathan explained that the potato not only stopped bleeding but also the starch soaked out the infection.

To take care of her cuts now, Miriam scratched a potato with her nails until she had enough gratings to cover the wound. Then she molded the pulp against her skin, wrapped it with a leaf and tied the dressing with a long, narrow plant stem. If the sore stayed, as her foot wounds often did now, she changed the potato compresses five or six times a day.

Miriam's isolation from people was becoming dangerous to her because she didn't realize how self-absorbed she was. Intent only on her survival, she didn't notice or even look for signs of activity around her.

She had just dug up a potato and was still on her hands and knees when she was jerked to her feet by a rough hand on the back of her shirt. She threw her arms and legs violently, trying to get away, but the red-faced farmer didn't let go.

"You taking my potatoes? You're no hungrier than the rest of us, but if you want a potato, take it."

He shoved a potato into Miriam's mouth and pushed it part way down her throat. At first she coughed and then the potato closed her throat and she couldn't breathe. He pulled the potato out of her mouth and said, "Do you still want a potato?"

Miriam didn't answer.

"Well girl, tell me, do you still want a potato?" He held her with one hand and lifted the potato to her mouth again with the other.

Miriam shook her head back and forth, not speaking but trying to escape.

"So I guess you don't want no more potatoes. Got your fill this time. Come around again and I'll shove this potato down your throat and leave it there.

He dropped her to the ground and she scrambled away as he shouted, "Girl, I'm lettin' you go. I gave you the potato you wanted and now I'm lettin' you go. You ain't no more hungry than the rest of us."

Now, Miriam was afraid to take potatoes but she worried her sores would get infected. She remembered her father saying plants that cover the ground can also cover the body. He showed her a plant low to the ground with wide, green leaves full of thick veins and told her these plantain leaves healed sores. Potatoes were easier to use but these crushed leaves could do just as well.

She found the plants, picked the leaves and took them to the nearest water. After she washed the leaves, she tore them to make sure the veins were broken. When juice from the veins moistened the leaves, she bound the wound with the mixture and tied the wrapping with cedar bark that she soaked at the same time.

The cedar bark was strong. She cut it apart with a sharp rock, but once it was wet, it got soft and stringy. She made a cord and tied it around the wound. Then, she put another layer of the plantain leaf over the wrapping and started again. This double protection insured no dirt would get under the first leaf poultice. Each time she prepared the covering, she washed the leaf and the sore, replacing the leaves until the wound closed. Miriam didn't need people and she didn't need their potatoes. The forest would give her everything.

Now, even when she was thirsty, she stayed in the forest and sucked the juice of clover rather than go out to the ponds and lakes. She searched for a special lavender flower, the one her father picked for her on their hikes together.

"People think a flower's value is in its beauty and its fragrance," he told her, "but a flower offers much more. It can have a juice tasting better than any drink and giving energy too." When he picked the flower, right at the place where it met the stem, he did it gently, so as not to lose the sap. Then cupping the flower with both hands, he brought it flush against his lips and sucked.

When Nathan gave one to Miriam, she sucked, but the petals were smooth and dry against her lips. "You're not sucking hard enough," he encouraged. "You need to suck in as hard as you can to force the flower to release its moisture. It's nature's way for the flower to protect itself. You need to overpower it."

He told her that the clover flower did more than quench thirst. The sweetness she tasted gave energy like sugar. The flower was as nourishing as her mother's beef broth with garlic. He wanted her to be able to tell it apart from other purple flowers.

When Miriam found the flower, she sucked with all her strength until her lungs hurt. She thought it was impossible for juice to flow from the petals, hundreds of tiny pieces which looked more like seeds than petals. Her father told her to suck harder but she never tasted the juice. Now, it flowed into her mouth, and, as it did, an energy traveled through her body.

In the spring, the forest gave her clover whenever she needed it. It gave her other food too. The hawthorn trees with their reddish brown bark would bloom full white flowers and she would watch them turn into a hard, scarlet berry. When these haws were ripe, she'd eat them, and not just for their taste. They settled her stomach and relaxed her. In late spring, she made a sandwich, squeezing the haws between the hawthorn leaves. These sandwiches were delicacies because the hawthorn tree was short, only 16 feet, more like a bush than a tree, but was well protected by its prominent thorns. Miriam picked between the thorns to get the berries. Beechnuts weren't as tasty but they were easier to harvest, falling from their trees and waiting for her to find them under the trunks. If she was lucky, she found crabapples or maybe even rosehips. She ate the rosehips, even when they weren't fully ripe and were still bitter. Rosehips were good for her, her father said, giving her vitamins she needed.

Miriam sucked three more clover flowers and then she began to walk. The forest was the only home she trusted.

CHAPTER EIGHT

September 1944
Four trains of Jews travel from Holland to
Auschwitz. Almost everyone on the train is
gassed, including children. Most likely, Ann
Frank, whose parents brought her to
Holland as a refugee before the War, is one
of these children.

In the forest, Miriam's imagination protected her from her fear of the war. Noise from bombs and artillery again filled the air but Miriam didn't hear them. She heard the music of the woods. Her life songs were the wind blowing leaves against each other and nightingales serenading her with her mother's mournful melodies. She didn't hear anything else, not even her own murmurings. She became her mother's child, lapsing into a world of unconscious humming and creating comfort in her own music.

Rarely now, she thought about her home and her parents in Vilna. More and more, she talked to the trees. She lost her family in the small clearing when the farmer surprised her, releasing her family dreams when the farmer released his grip on her shoulder. Her family was the forest and she thought now that she belonged here. The odors of decaying wood and leaf mold were familiar companions. At first, the smells were like a strong stench, but now she missed them when she left the woods and welcomed their message that the forest was alive, well and regenerating itself when she returned.

The early evening was quiet. The nightingales, wood warblers and blackcaps stopped their chorus. Later, the eagle owls, great grey owls and pigmy owls flew through the trees and swooped down for mice. Their flights made a recognizable swoosh through the night air. Miriam walked in figure eight circles waiting for the sunrise to tell her to stop. No matter what her mind did, Miriam's body continued the ritual and practice of movement. To stop was to die. Her body knew to keep going.

The noises of morning were her signal to rest, but this morning the sounds were different. Planes flew over the trees but the usual explosions didn't follow the fading engines. Instead, flutters of paper accompanied each dive over the forest. Miriam picked up one and read the Polish, Russian and Yiddish. The letters were large and bold, filling the page with the words. "The war is over. Come out of the woods."

She didn't know why there were so many papers. She rarely saw anyone in the forest now. She read flyers before. They said, "Don't run away. Come out. The Germans left." Some people believed the papers because they wanted to. When they walked to a clearing, soldiers were waiting, like a firing squad, to shoot them. Miriam never believed the papers. She didn't believe these either. When the papers fell again, she retreated deeper into the forest.

Then, the planes stopped. The bombs stopped and so did the artillery, but Miriam didn't notice their silence until days later. Her blocking out these sounds was so successful that she eliminated them. She had to listen for the plane noise to realize it was gone.

When the planes came again, they dropped packages, not bombs or papers. Miriam opened one. It was filled with dried food, but she didn't eat any because she thought that the contents were poisoned. She stayed closer to the forest's edge, and for the first time in months, she saw other people in the forest. She watched them open the boxes and eat what was inside. Finally she ate too, very slowly, and making sure she drank water first.

The dried meat in the package was hard, more like the straw and molasses fed to horses. She chewed and chewed until her teeth ached. In one day, her body had a different energy. She decided she would do anything to keep it.

The day after she ate, she heard voices from loud speakers. "We are coming to take you where there is food and clothes. The war is finished."

The words got louder and louder until she thought they were being shouted to her. When they were all she could hear, she walked toward the sound. A horse and buggy appeared beside her. The horse stopped, and the man with the megaphone motioned her to get on but she didn't move. He, and another man, jumped from the buggy and lifted her under the arms onto the buggy floor. When she didn't sit down, one of them touched her on the shoulder and gently pushed downward.

The horse had no path to follow and the ride through the forest was rough. Each bump jarred her memory. "Sonia, where are we going and how will we get there? Sonia, tell Lisper to slow down. Sonia, hold me." The memories came too fast, rushing over her and flooding the present with past.

"Turn back Sonia. It's not too late."

"Speak in Russian. We don't understand," one of the men said.

The other man said, "I think she's telling you to turn back. I understand some Polish."

"Tell her we can't turn back. Tell her we're taking her where there's food."

"My heart is broke," she answered in Russian. "I have no heart to follow. I don't know where to go."

The man continued as if he didn't realize she understood Russian. "Tell the little Jewish girl she's going with us. I can't make anything of what she's saying. She's one of the youngest we've found so far, and she's alone too. Do you think she knows who she is? "

"Miriam. My name is Miriam Kornitsky."

If he knew she was Jewish, she needn't hide her name.

"Well, Miriam, we're taking you where there's food. No need to worry now."

The walls of the room were lined with stove after stove. Big soup pots of water boiled on their burners. Wooden tubs covered the floor space. Nurses, or women Miriam thought were nurses because of their white outfits, spoke in different languages, until one worked, telling women to remove their clothes.

A nurse took Miriam's pants as soon as they were off, but Miriam grabbed them back.

"We'll give you another pair, Miriam. You said your name was Miriam, didn't you? There are no death walks here. You'll get better clothes, believe me."

Miriam made no sense from the conversation. She knew nothing of death walks. But she watched other women in the room take off their clothes, and she saw they removed them with both anxiety and resignation. Miriam didn't fear the bath, but she didn't let loose of the pants when the nurse asked for them the second time. After turning the pants inside out, she lifted up the pocket lining and bit a hole through it. She stuck a finger through the hole and poked until she hit a hard round object, pushing another finger through so she could get hold of the hard metal object and maneuver it through the hole. The ring was more black than gold, covered with the rich forest soil of her journey. Its weight in her palm was an anchor to the past. She rubbed her fingers across it as if it were shiny and smooth.

"My parents gave it to me, my parents in Vilna."

The nurse took her pants and helped her remove her other clothes. Turning her blouse inside out, Miriam tore a cotton patch from the front panel. Between the two layers was a picture of her mother and father, Rebecca and Nathan, posed in a formal portrait. The edges were torn but the faces were still intact. Miriam hadn't looked at the photograph since her foray into the small village when she was caught by the farmer outside his cabin. Her family had died then and now they came back to her.

"My parents," she said to the nurse. "Perhaps you know of them. In Vilna. I'm from Vilna." She spoke as if years hadn't passed.

Miriam stood nude against the wooden tub, holding the ring and the picture, and questioning the nurse.

Miriam wasn't the first to come through this room, asking these questions. Most everyone asked the aide the same questions; she didn't know if they expected answers, but usually they stopped asking her when she shook her head and, instead, they talked to each other. Miriam kept asking.

"My parents would want me to come to them. Do you know where they are?"

"Miriam, you are in Russia. When you're strong and ready, you can go back to Vilna. Now you need to take a bath, to get clean so that you don't get sick."

"I am clean. My father told me to stay clean. You'll see, I'm clean."

Miriam stepped into the tub but a different woman walked over to wash her, and the nurse who took her clothes didn't come back. The water was lukewarm, not scalding as she had expected, and the nurse rubbed firmly but the pressure was soothing to her skin. When the nurse put her hand on Miriam's shoulder, Miriam sucked in a breath and waited to be pushed under. Instead, the nurse talked to her.

"Your hair needs to be washed. If you get your head wet, it will be easier to soap. Then I'll rinse you with a pitcher. You'll be through except for the spraying."

The spray was a fine white mist of powder squirted to hit every part of the body. It tickled her stomach and the inside of her thighs. The nurse asked Miriam to sit down and lift her legs so the bottom of her feet could be sprayed. The DDT powder, used to kill lice, irritated skin but Miriam didn't know so she didn't connect the spraying to her itching and burning the next day.

"Now, you'll have these clothes until we find ones better suited for you." The nurse handed Miriam a man's shirt and boy's trousers. "You'll find food in the next room and someone will tell you where to go after that."

90

Miriam followed the directions without a question, walking to the door just as if she were walking to the forest's edge. They gave her boy's pants. Her mother would not be pleased.

The tables in the room were piled with breads, meats, cheeses and fruits. Clothes couldn't cover the emptiness of the shapeless figures along the tables, and the feast couldn't restore emaciated bodies. The food wasn't suited to the starving survivors any better than the clothes.

Miriam looked at the food and her stomach turned, in remembrance of the table in Luba. She saw red Jell-O in a glass bowl at the end of the table. She'd eat a little and let her stomach stretch.

Today, she'd eat the Jell-O and tomorrow she'd eat some bread and fruit. She saw the cottage cheese but didn't touch it. She wouldn't eat dairy until she could hold soup and meat.

Someone at a table across from hers yelled, "I have pains, horrible pains here," and pointed to his stomach. Then he fell to the floor. Miriam waited for him to roll over and gasp for air. Instead, he simply stopped breathing. Two soldiers carried the body away. He weighed so little that each used only one hand to carry him and still he was well about their shoulders. Others died, the same evening, in the dining area.

Those who sat in the hall could have been sitting shiva, mourning losses, but no wails or sobs followed these deaths. The room had no celebrations and it had no sorrows, but the people were mourners nevertheless, waiting to be taken back to life.

Doctors learned later that the very food served to the survivors with such good intent had killed the weakest of them. It was like poison to people whose stomachs forgot how to produce what was needed to digest nutrients but whose hunger demanded they take in as much as they could. Even too much liquid could make a stomach explode, but few knew of the consequences then.

Miriam watched the deaths but didn't see them. Dying had lost its meaning just as life no longer had a definition.

She sat at the table until someone led her to another room, a room of cots and bunk beds pushed so close together that she walked sideways to get through. Over half the beds were taken. Women lay curled up in cots that didn't bulge underneath and in bunk beds that didn't sway. A few children slept in beds with their mothers but even then, the mattresses did not protest the weight. A mother and child together did not weigh enough to sink the cotton material of the cot. And no one had the energy to toss and turn.

Miriam didn't stop at the first empty bed. When the woman leading her realized Miriam was not going to choose for herself , she selected a location and guided her to a cot. "You'll sleep here tonight."

She curled up like the others, becoming one of them and, without the noise of leaves brushing against each other, fell asleep.

The next day, Miriam saw herself in a mirror. The reflection looked like the hundreds of others in the camp with no faces and no bodies, only heads, eyes and swollen legs. She survived by herself, listened only to herself but now she was the same as the others.

The organizers of the camp set the activities of the day. When they put food on the tables, people ate. When they prepared the water, people took baths. And when they handed out clothes, the men and women changed into them.

Either the survivors in the camp did not talk at all, like Miriam, or they talked all the time. After a week, the quiet of the first days changed to a constant drone. People talked through the night, and their exhaustion was replaced with a restlessness that had people walking around at all hours.

Miriam stuck to a routine, doing everything to make herself ready for the trip back to her parents. She talked to them. "When I get home, you'll see how well I've done. I'm eating cottage cheese now and my stomach muscles are growing. Papa, I don't belong with these people. I want to be with you and Mama. I take long walks into the forest but I always come back here. I'm afraid to leave but soon I have to. Papa, where will I go and how will I get there?"

Finally, instead of imaginary conversations with her parents, she asked the nurse a question. "Where am I?"

It took her a month to ask.

"You're in Russia on the outskirts of a small town, Novosokolniki. These barracks were used for soldiers and then abandoned when the Germans invaded. We have no military need for them now. We pushed the Germans back and our soldiers are even farther west."

"I was in Glubokoye. I can remember it." Miriam's response didn't make sense to the nurse but she was used to these conversations and tried to continue them.

"Where?"

"In Glubokoye."

"In Russia?"

93

"No, in Poland. I live in Vilna. I walked very far and I remember it was Glubokoye."

"I've heard people say you'll be going back soon."

"I am? You heard someone tell you that?"

"The group, the whole group will be sent back. We can't take care of you here."

Sent back. That afternoon, Miriam looked in the mirror and again saw someone she didn't know. Her body was filling out. They were giving her skirts at the distribution center, as they gave the other women, and now she saw that she had the body of a woman.

In the camp, whenever Miriam was puzzled, she took a walk in the nearby woods. She was returning from a walk the afternoon a Russian soldier grabbed her arm. Holding her around the throat with one hand, he pressed his other against her abdomen, pulled it up along her stomach and stopped at her breasts. With his hand clutching her breast, he declared, "We saved Jew women and we should have them." He moved his hand from Miriam's breast to her buttocks. "Now there's a bottom for someone, a nice, firm and lean one. It got that way on our food."

Miriam didn't resist; she didn't have it in her to fight.

The soldier ran his fingers over her chin and along her throat to her collar. Then he ripped open her cotton blouse, stripping the coarse material from her body. She didn't raise a hand to cover her breasts or defend herself. She was like a doll, a mannequin of flesh and bone.

He caressed one breast, first with his fingertips and then with the palm of his hand. Still she didn't move.

The soldier let go of her arm, putting both palms on her chest; he pressed hard and then pushed her away. "You Jew girls might as well be dead for all the good you'll do us."

Miriam walked back to the barracks; she could not run, just as she could not fight. She didn't get a different blouse until the next morning, and she didn't tell anyone what happened. She didn't have anyone to tell. Curled up on her cot, she talked to her mother as if Rebecca were there with her. "Mama, I don't want to be a lady."

Her father didn't tell her what do when she became a woman. She wasn't afraid of men when she left the forest, but now she avoided the Russian soldiers.

In the dining area, she overheard people talking about trains leaving from Velikijo Luki, 20 kilometers west of the camp. Nobody said where the trains were going and nobody asked her if she wanted to go home. She would go to Velikijo Luki and take the train.

The camp stopped serving meat a month before. Bread, stiff black bread difficult to digest, and hard thin slices of cheese were on the tables. She wrapped them both in a cloth, the only item she carried with her as she left the camp, except for the ring in her pocket and her parent's picture now stitched between the folds of her skirt.

No one kept records on the people in the camp so she wouldn't be missed. In fact, Miriam hardly recognized the faces there from day to day. People left even before they looked able to walk, even though they knew the distance to the station and knew it could be days before a train appeared. Miriam decided it was better to gain weight and strength before starting the trip back. She overheard stories about the trains from people who returned because they couldn't get food or water in Velikijo Luki while they camped out, waiting for a train or, by the time the train came, they didn't have enough food and water to survive the ride. Weaker survivors died at the station, waiting for trains to arrive, and some passengers died on the trains, committed to leaving whether they were ready or not. When Miriam left, she was ready for the trip.

She started for Velikijo Luki, walking from the camp to the road in the daylight. People were wandering the streets, those who had no place to go, like her, and those who had nothing to do, like the soldiers. She heard two soldiers in worn, brown uniforms discussing the body of a woman who was walking a few feet ahead. Miriam wished she didn't understand Russian.

"Her rear is small. Will we have anything to hold on to?"

"I'll hold her for you, don't worry," the taller soldier said. "We have our pick but she's the best I see."

The other soldier looked around as if to verify the observation. "You're right. I like the way she moves. We'll have her."

They walked up to her, each on a side, and put their hands under her armpits. They carried her along for about twenty meters into an area encircled by trees but still visible to people nearby. Those who saw the soldiers approach the woman kept walking and others who could see through the trees into the clearing did not stop to watch. As if fixed in position, being forced not to move, Miriam saw the soldiers rape the woman.

The taller one pulled at the babushka tied around the woman's head and held her arms, as he said he would, while the other tore open her blouse. Then the first soldier released her arms and cupped his hands over her breasts, holding her tightly. His friend untied the knot of his roped sash and his baggy army pants fell over his black boots. He lifted the woman's skirt and motioned for his friend to hold it up. Then he put a hand on the inside of each thigh and pushed them apart. With his hands pressing against her thighs, he thrust himself joylessly against the woman. His friend watched, waiting his turn, while he held his grip on the woman's skirt and breasts.

The first soldier took his hands from her thighs and pulled up his pants in a single motion. Then he picked up his sash and tied it around his tunic. When his clothes were in place, he signaled his friend to release her and reached to grab her arms, to hold her in place for his companion. The taller soldier took his hand from her breast and wrapped it around her waist but then he let go.

"It's enough," he said to the other soldier.

The woman, who had not spoken until now, said in clear Russian, "I want money from you."

The soldiers laughed.

"We picked a Russian one," the smaller man laughed. He laughed again, stuck his hand in a pocket, and put the coin he pulled out in the woman's outstretched palm.

The soldiers walked back to the road and the woman followed soon after. Miriam walked toward the trees into the small clearing. It was as if no one had been there and when she looked toward the road, she didn't see the woman or the soldiers. She walked back to camp.

She had no one to say hello to when she got back and she didn't have anyone to say good-bye to when she left again that evening.

This time, she followed the road and although she didn't see the trees alongside, they were her companions for the journey. The night became her friend, too, a protector from the threats and fears of daytime. Russian soldiers didn't look for a girl on the road at night. In the daytime, they might take her off the road and into the woods or even twenty meters to the side of the road behind some large trees. No matter that witnesses would see the abduction. The day was unsafe more than the night, just as Sonia said it would be. Still, the afternoon was in another kind of darkness. People walked with their hands down and their shoulders sloped forward. It was as if they couldn't see anything and the sky was in its blackest night.

Now, in the dark of evening, Miriam passed the clearing where the soldiers took the Russian woman. She knew the location but didn't want to remember what she saw there. Instead, she thought of the Russian soldier who lifted her onto the horse and buggy in the woods. With his dark hair and black moustache, his face, for an instant, had been a portrait of her father. The night cleared her thoughts. In her mind, she saw the direction of Velikijo Luki and from it, the way home.

She walked for hours without stopping. Her leg muscles ached and her shoes rubbed blisters on her toes. Miriam wasn't used to long hours on her feet anymore. She saw people sleeping along the road but decided not to rest. The night was for moving. She arrived in Velikijo Luki exhausted

The sky lightened just as she approached the outskirts of the town. The summer morning arrived without a sunrise, a gray welcome to the city, but Miriam didn't notice bleakness because she was going somewhere. No more uncertain figure eight circles in the forest. Every step, every movement was toward Vilna.

The small farms off the road were like those she visited from the forest. The need to belong somewhere and the loneliness that overtook her then were fragments of a past journey. Now, even the morning smoke from the chimneys didn't tempt her toward the farms. She no longer cared what was happening in front of those fireplaces; they had nothing to offer. Walking along the road, away from the farmhouses, Miriam joined others. They were going home. She was going home.

"Follow the Oshmyany Minsk Road toward Russia but be in the forest by morning." She overheard the directions to Sonia and remembered the people who traveled the edges of the forest. They were herded like sheep by aerial snipers who circled and then attacked. Bodies lined the side of the road. She thought of them now because this morning, bodies also lined the roadside, resting before they moved on toward the city.

Miriam didn't talk to these people along the road. She talked to her father. "Papa, I have to follow them because they are returning as I am. Lisper and Sonia cannot leave the forest, but I'll be in the city by morning."

The train station was easy to find because everyone was going there. It looked like the camp she left, without the barracks. People put together makeshift tents from tree limbs and odd pieces of clothing. Talk was incessant, but conversations were short.

"I'm from Warsaw and my family name is Goldinsky. My brothers are Sam and Ben and my mother is Esther. Maybe somewhere you'll see them. Tell them Eli is alive."

"I'm from Lublin and the family name is Kinburg, Kinburg – we are five children, Sarah, Benjamin, Ruth, Jacob and Sophie."

"I'm Jacob Lansky from Glubokoye. We are five brothers, all married with children. Lansky from Glubokoye."

"Glubokoye, I was in Glubokoye."

Miriam shook her head at each person who approached and they quickly moved on, but Glubokoye was different. She had been there.

"Any Lansky's, any Lansky's at all in Glubokoye?" He pressed for information but Miriam couldn't think of any to give. Just finding someone who had been in the town was enough for the man to continue.

"No one was in Glubokoye," she said finally. "I was afraid in Glubokoye."

"No one in Glubokoye?"

"I saw dead bodies in the forest, by Glubokoye."

The man wanted to know what the bodies looked like, what clothes they had on, what jewelry they were wearing. She shook her head to each demand and finally he went on.

Miriam turned to the person next to her, an old man sitting on the ground with his head in his hands.

"I'm Miriam Kornitsky from Vilna. Jacob, my brother was taken by soldiers to Russia, Jacob Kornitsky."

He didn't lift his head. She went to the next man.

"I'm Miriam from Vilna. My family name is Kornitsky, Nathan and Rebecca are my parents."

He shook his head and she went on. Suddenly, the need to know became as important as the desire to find someone. Velikijo Luki was not the place to get information but she didn't know that. For her, it was the beginning.

No train came that day, or the next. Miriam ate her bread and cheese, breaking it up into small pieces because she didn't know how long it would have to last. Her stomach was used to camp rations and the hunger pangs of an empty stomach brought back unwelcomed sensations.

Now, when she had doubts, she talked to her father, her almost constant companion.

"Papa, I know the forest has food but I don't want to leave here. What if the train should come while I'm gone and then when would there be another? I have to stay."

She stopped asking about her family, not giving up but realizing that whoever these people were, none traveled more than she, and she had no information to offer anyone. Others continued to ask, over and over.

"Lansky, Lansky from Glubokoye. We are five brothers, all married with children."

Miriam shook her head and he moved on, without any recognition that he had questioned her before.

These people didn't know where they were going yet she was choosing to travel with them. She explained out loud, "Papa, where am I to go? I must follow or I'll never get home."

Sticking her hand in a pocket, she rolled her fingers around the ring covered by the cotton lining and sang to herself, "Where loving arms will lift me close and guide a child who's gone astray." She worked the hard metal between her fingers until they ached.

On the third day, the train came. Boxcars, one after another, fifteen of them, lined the tracks. People who had been unable to move five minutes before, rushed the cars. At first they tried to sit on the floors but the cars were too crowded and people on the bottom were trampled. Miriam walked beside the track, from car to car, hoping to find one less crowded. Others were afraid to give up what they knew they had and the first cars were packed like cattle trains. Miriam walked past thirteen cars before she saw one that had room to sit.

Hundreds of people got on the train; none knew where it was going. Once it started, none knew when it would stop. The train was headed west and for them, that was enough.

Miriam rocked with the motion of the train. "I won't have to jump this one, Papa."

Miriam was sure this train would take her to Vilna.

CHAPTER NINE

*The number of Jews killed in Europe
between September 1939 and May 1945 is
nearly six million. Almost two million
survive, 300,000 from the concentration
camps and one and half million who escape
before the War or who are saved by the
courage of people like the Danes.*

Miriam could get on any train she wanted and then get off whenever or wherever it stopped. No one asked for a ticket; no one offered a schedule; and no one announced a destination. At least, she was moving. And in her mind, she was moving toward Vilna.

The train from Velikijo Luki stopped at Vitebsk. Russian soldiers were stationed at the stop, and somehow passengers knew not to fear them. In fact, the soldiers were there to take refugees to a camp. Miriam had no reason to think this camp would be different from the one she left, but she understood Russian and the soldiers said anyone who went with them would have a good meal.

In truth, no one knew what to do with these war refugees, and Russian communities did not want them wandering the streets or sleeping in the fields of the countryside. They tried to entice survivors of the war into displaced person camps with promises of food and shelter. At first, it was enough.

Miriam was hungry so she went with the soldiers, but after they escorted her and other willing passengers, she never saw them again. She also never saw anyone she could say was organizing the camp, but the one meal a day was always served at the same time in the late afternoon. And it was always the same – Russian rations the refugees called them – two slices of hard, brown bread; a bowl of soup, more broth than substance; and a scoop of kasha, a brown grain mixed with fat and spices. Miriam ate what was served but missed the green plants and fresh berries of the forest. "I don't have a choice of what is best for me to eat," she said aloud while she was picking up the bread to dip in the soup. After years by herself, she was still telling her father why she did something against his advice.

Miriam's identification card, issued to her at the first camp, allowed her to stay in this camp at night, but each day she'd go to the station to wait for the next train. She saw hundreds of people by the tracks. No trains were coming and the Russians weren't letting people into the camps anymore. Soldiers handed out food in the early afternoon, but the rations were never enough. Even then, refugees fended for themselves to find shelter or a safe place to sleep. These people with no place to go were waiting for trains to take them somewhere, anywhere.

Miriam wandered back and forth from the camp to the station, sometimes sleeping at the station for fear she'd miss the train if it came at night. Her journey back and forth was no burden for she had nothing to carry except the papers issued by the camp allowing her food rations and a place to sleep. If she stayed at the station at night, she might have no food. Some late afternoons, Polish volunteers set up stands to serve a hot broth, but Miriam might stand in line for hours only to find an empty pot at the end of her wait. Others, who had no ration or ID cards, were selling their meager possessions to sympathetic passersby so they could buy food. A shirt could bring 50 zloty and family jewelry much more. Six zloty bought an egg, but the money couldn't buy a ticket out of Vitebsk so Miriam didn't care that she had nothing to sell. When she was hungry, she watched the bartering and fingered her mother's wedding ring. The ring was all she had until she got to Vilna. She'd never sell it.

It was a month before the next train stopped in Vitebsk. When Miriam heard about the train – people in the camp somehow knew of its arrival two hours before it came – she took her bread ration and left. Only a dozen or so people left with her. The rest were satisfied with food and a place to stay.

She didn't know the train's destination, but at least it was going somewhere. She didn't get off when the train stopped in small towns because she didn't know how long it would be before it started again and, if it left without her, the next one could be days, weeks or even a month away. When the train stopped in Minsk, the name repeated like an echo throughout the cars. Miriam didn't know Minsk, but everyone got off when the train stopped, so she went with them.

Soldiers at the station were shouting instructions. "Go register and get your ration card. Even if you have a ration card from somewhere else, you need a new one."

Miriam walked through the streets, part of the sea of refugees who ultimately formed yet another line in which to wait. The street was edged with half-standing buildings. Papers were flying everywhere, shevuot, torn scraps in Hebrew from the pages of prayer books. After five hours in line, she moved forward enough to see a wooden sign above the door of a large red building. Painted on it in tar, and in many languages, was "UNRRA, Registration." Registration she knew. UNRRA were meaningless letters. Soon, she would come to learn how important they would be: UNRRA, United Nations Refugee Relief Agency.

Inside the building were thick pads of paper, page after page of names, dates and cities. She signed her name, "Miriam Kornitsky," and her city, "Vilna," but she had to ask the date. Miriam stopped writing when she heard the reply, "July 1, 1945." I am 17 years old, Miriam thought to herself. She wanted to stay for hours, searching the lists for the name Kornitsky but the Russians in charge kept announcing people had fifteen minutes to look at the list and then a new group had to be let in. She found a Jacob Rabinsky from Vilna but he signed the book in April.

Officials sent people to another room to be issued identification cards, which they said would work anywhere in Poland. When Miriam left the building with hers, she saw people with signs attached to their shirts: " Joseph Minsk, Warsaw " "Rose Shapiro, Bobrujsk" "Nathan Schatopsky, Krakow." The small identification cards didn't communicate what people on the streets needed to tell each other so they wore signs. "Here's who I am. Do you know or have you seen anyone with my last name?"

Miriam found a piece of paper and wrote "Miriam Kornitsky, Vilna" and pushed a hole through the paper so she could button it to her blouse.

Everyday people performed the same ritual. They walked the streets of Minsk with their signs, hoping someone would recognize a name or a city and then tell stories about the family. After Miriam walked for hours, she would wait in line for hours to check the new lists in the registration building. She had no more luck than if she had been in Velikijo Luki.

Two weeks of searching in Minsk was enough. Miriam had to get closer to Vilna, although she had no idea where closer was or how she would get there. She did know that trains left often from Minsk, and, again, no one seemed to need a ticket. While she was prepared for a long journey, the ride was only a few hours. The train stopped in Bobrujsk, and two men wearing civilian clothes said everyone had to leave the cars. Miriam waited for hours to register at the UNRRA center in Bobrujsk but, in the scribbled list of all the people who came before her, she didn't see any names from Vilna.

The next train stopped in Lida. Miriam was familiar with the name. Rarely, did she travel with her parents anywhere but to Vilna's town center, and then only infrequently, but she heard them talk about Lida. In fact, Lida was just one hundred kilometers from Vilna but Miriam didn't know. Still, she didn't leave the car to visit the UNRRA center, even though she was sure Lida had one. Trains came unannounced and left unannounced with no one knowing when the next would appear. If her parents talked about Lida, then she was close to home.

The train stayed on the Lida tracks for three days. If a soup station was set up next to her car, Miriam got off to eat something, but only if she was one of the first in line. Otherwise, she didn't leave the train for three days.

One evening, she woke to the sound of train engines revving up. Slowly, the train built momentum and soon, she saw only countryside from her window. Miriam was on her way to Vilna. She knew it, even though the destination was not announced.

And she was right. The train stopped in Vilna, but not the Vilna she remembered traveling to with her father, not the Vilna market where her father sold his meager products when the fields and the weather were good to him.

The Vilna she came to in 1945 was a destroyed city. Buildings were rubble, at least in the Jewish section, and people said the countryside was worse. Just because the war was over didn't mean the Poles were welcoming Jews back. Poles had taken the empty farmhouses and were working the abandoned land. Refugees who returned to claim property were a threat.

Miriam, the child, returned a young woman in desperate search of brothers who would be men and in search of parents who might not recognize her but would be so proud, especially her father, once they knew how she survived by listening to them.

Her long wait in the UNNRA line brought success. Miriam found her brother's name handwritten on the list. "Joseph Kornitsky," May 1945, Vilna. Joseph was there; she only had to find him.

For two days, she walked Mitschkivicha, the main street of Vilna, wearing a paper buttoned to her shirt with the name, "Kornitsky" in big letters. And, not giving anyone the opportunity to ignore her, she went to each person on the street and asked, "Do you know Joseph Kornitsky? Have you seen Joseph Kornitsky?"

The city of Vilna was as strange to her as Minsk for she had rarely gone into town as a child. Only the outdoor market where her father sold his fruit would have been familiar, but Vilna had no outdoor market now. For two days, she slept in a converted bunker and used her ration card to get bread and vegetable soup. Vilna food lines had no meat.

In some ways, now, she was dependent upon the anonymous benefactors who gave her a ration card and provided her daily meals. Although she wanted more than anything to find Joseph and to be in her house again, she was frightened to leave the city of Vilna. It wasn't until the third day, when she hadn't found anyone who knew or saw Joseph, that she walked the 10 kilometers to the farmhouse.

A kilometer before she reached the house, a man working in an apple orchard saw and stopped her.

"You're one of those coming back, aren't you?"

"I'm Miriam Kornitsky and I'm looking for my family. My parents are Rebecca and Nathan. We live in the farmhouse down the road. I'm looking for my brother, Joseph who was in Vilna two months ago."

"You lived in that house about a kilometer down?"

"Yes."

"And your brother was here two months ago?"

"Yes, he was here, I'm sure."

"Then he was the one. He was walking through the house when a sniper got him through the window. Got him in the head and he was dead when the Walesky's found him."

He relayed the information as if filing a news report, with no accommodation for the young woman who was hearing that her brother was murdered by a stranger for no apparent reason.

Miriam was sure he was describing some other person. No one would kill her brother in his own house. If she just asked more questions, she would find out that he was wrong.

"The Walesky's?"

"The family that has the house now. They buried him down by the river, but they didn't know who he was. He was one of the first ones here."

Miriam tried one more time. In a desperate voice, low and hesitant, she said, "I know it couldn't be my brother. How could someone kill my brother in his own house?"

Answering with a tone of indifference but providing his perspective, he said, "He got killed in the Walesky house. Maybe somebody thought he was looting."

Miriam wanted to ask questions about her parents. She wanted to know where they went and if anyone had seen them, but she couldn't ask him. She couldn't believe him. He said her house belonged to someone else. He said that her brother was dead. She didn't want to talk to him. She would go to her farmhouse and find her brother.

Miriam turned away, not wanting this stranger to see her cry, but she cried all the way to the farmhouse. The house was a blur through her tears but when she saw it, she stopped. Miriam looked at the window of the stone house and saw her brother behind it. She turned around and walked back toward Vilna. Miriam knew the vision of Joseph's face was her wish for him to be alive, but when she looked at the house, she knew the truth. Joseph was dead.

But her parents could not be dead. Her father was stronger than she. Surely, he protected her mother and used every skill to survive that he taught her. Because she needed to know they were alive, she stopped again to ask the man in the

110

orchard about her parents. She didn't want to talk to him, this man who told a sister that her brother was killed as if he were talking to a stranger about a stranger. Yet, when she passed, she shouted, "My parents. Do you know about my parents, Rebecca and Nathan Kornitsky?"

"Nobody's been here except you and that fellow got shot," he said.

Miriam did not mourn her brother, at least so that the man could see. Her years in the forest froze her outward emotions. She turned without asking more questions, walked back to Vilna, to the station, and climbed the metal steps into the first train she saw. When the train left the tracks and Vilna disappeared from view, sobs escaped from her tightly shut mouth and tears poured down her cheeks. They came as rapidly and as uncontrollably as they had in the metal tub in Luba when Wlodek threw soap in her eyes. And they stopped just as suddenly. Miriam knew she would find her parents. Somewhere, they were waiting for her.

CHAPTER TEN

April 1945
Hitler commits suicide. A month later,
Germany surrenders, marking the end of
the Third Reich.

The train delivered Miriam to Disna, a place no different from other mystery cities in this strange tour of unwanted stops, except in one way. Food lines were in small grocery stores. Refugees could use their ration cards in certain of these shops designated as distribution centers. Although anyone could purchase food from these same stores, most citizens avoided the shops that served the refugees.

The second day in Disna, Miriam found herself nudged and pushed by other refugees standing in line at one of these groceries. Survivors were not a patient people, but Miriam was different. She did not shove back. She stood still in line, clutching her food vouchers in both hands as if she expected someone to grab them from her at any time. She stood quietly, without moving, but her eyes darted everywhere, searching the store, looking for nothing.

A young woman, also in line, was watching Miriam. Her parents told her to avoid the stores that distributed food parcels to the surviving Jews, but she was just past seventeen and her curiosity was stronger than their advice. She didn't know why she was drawn to Miriam, but she was. She stared at her, fascinated by this woman who wasn't even aware that she was the subject of such interest. The longer she looked, the more she noticed how unaware Miriam was of the people in the store or of the events around her. Miriam's eyes were moving constantly but the young woman soon realized the movements were too fast to focus on anything or anyone. Miriam moved her eyes so that she wouldn't have to pay attention to anything or anyone around her. Still, the young woman hoped Miriam would notice her. When she didn't, the young woman moved close enough to brush Miriam with her shoulder. Miriam didn't respond.

The brown-eyed, black haired Russian teenager wanted to touch Miriam's blonde hair. Instead, she stood directly in front of Miriam and stared into her blue eyes and smiled, seeing for the first time that she and Miriam were close to the same age. Miriam didn't smile back but the young woman thought she saw her mouth waver ever so slightly as if to acknowledge her presence. The movement was enough for her. She threw both arms around Miriam's shoulders and hugged her, hugged her so tightly that Miriam would have found it difficult to break away. But Miriam did not try to break away. She bent into the hug and leaned her head against the young woman's neck. When Miriam did pull away, it was a deliberate yet reluctant act. She looked into the woman's dark eyes and perhaps saw the caring.

"My name is Sasha," the young woman said. "Sasha Sobolov."

In Russian as clear as Sasha's, Miriam said, "My name is Miriam, Miriam Kornitsky."

"I am taking you home, Miriam. I am making you my sister."

It was as simple as that.

Sasha took Miriam's hand and led her from the store. They held hands for the half-kilometer walk to Sasha's apartment, Sasha letting go only to turn the knob of the apartment door.

Miriam's new sister pulled her into the apartment with such exuberance that the food vouchers fell from Miriam's hands. She bent to get them, but Sasha didn't let go of her hands.

"It's for my food. I need them." Miriam's voice was soft but desperate.

Sasha quieted the fear in an immediate act of connection and commitment. "From now on, our food will be yours. You won't need those cards. You won't have to wait in line in those stores."

Sasha dropped Miriam's hand but only to free her own which she placed around Miriam's shoulder as she guided her in to the apartment.

Sasha brought Miriam to her mother in the kitchen. She told her that she found Miriam in a grocery store and that because she had no place to stay, Sasha brought her home to stay with them. Both Miriam and Sasha watched Mrs. Sobolov carefully for her reaction to this plan. Without hesitation, almost as if expecting Miriam to arrive, Mrs. Sobolov said Miriam was welcomed as long as she wanted to stay. She looked at Miriam while she spoke. "My daughter has been lonely since we left Russia. She needs a friend and I can see that you need one, too. I know my husband will feel the same. Accept our hospitality."

Miriam nodded her head but didn't say anything to Mrs. Sobolov. Sasha hugged her mother and then turned to Miriam. "See all the food we have in the kitchen. You won't need your cards. My mother has wonderful stuffed cabbage for lunch and she has started the peroki for dinner. We'll have some stuffed with cheese, some with potato and some with meat."

Miriam thought Sasha might be Jewish, although she wasn't sure why a Russian Jew would be in Poland. If Sasha's mother made rolled noodles stuffed with cheese and also meat at the same meal, then they weren't Jewish. Mixing meat and dairy wasn't kosher, wasn't within the dietary laws of the Jewish religion. In Vilna, most Jews kept kosher. Miriam had no way of knowing that many Jews in Russia no longer kept the dietary laws of their religion.

Miriam looked at the food in the kitchen and said, "I thought maybe you were Jewish."

"We are Jewish," Sasha answered.

"But you don't keep kosher. You're eating milk with meat tonight."

Sasha was surprised that Miriam thought they would do otherwise. "Only old fashioned Jews keep kosher," Sasha said.

"I wanted you to be Jewish," Miriam answered, not really interested in the practices of Jews in Russia.

Miriam was with the Sobolov family for a month and still told them little about herself. At first, they asked but when they realized she didn't want to talk, they stopped questioning. Even Sasha, who desperately wanted a friend, was satisfied with a quiet companion. Miriam did the chores

116

with her and sat by the fire with her when they finished. They drank strong, black Russian tea from fine porcelain cups and ate heavy apple strudel from the local Polish bakery.

Late, one quiet, chilly afternoon, as the fire played against Miriam's face, Sasha saw a heat from within Miriam more intense than the flames in the fireplace. She decided to break the accepted practice of silence. She was going to force Miriam to talk.

She set down her cup and put both hands on Miriam's thighs. Then she reached for Miriam's hand and held it while she spoke. "Miriam, it's time you talked. This burden of silence, it's as if you've made a pledge to destroy your feelings. Miriam, talk to me. Share the pains and make them less for you."

"My father said I shouldn't trust anyone but myself, Sasha. I want to talk to you but I can't."

"I'm not just curious. From the first time I saw you in line at the grocery, I knew that I was connected to you. I need to know what happened to you, and I know you need to tell me. Tell me now."

"Sasha, I've been alone for over three years..."

"And you'll be alone forever unless you free yourself. Talk to me. Begin now."

"If I tell you..."

"You won't have to tell it again."

"I won't have shown my father."

"Shown him what?"

"That I listened to him. He told me not to talk to anyone."

"He didn't mean me. Miriam, we're moving to Saltzheim, we're moving to Germany, and I want you to come with us. My parents know I've been lonely here and they're happy I've found a sister. They have a second daughter now, and they want to keep you, too."

Miriam used the announcement of the move as a reason, or perhaps an excuse, to stop this conversation with Sasha about her past. And she was quick to react to Sasha's statement. "I don't want to move. I will stay in Poland to find my parents and my brothers."

"We don't have a choice. The Russians have some say in the governing of Germany and they are sending officials to different cities. My father is assigned to Saltzheim."

"I don't speak German," Miriam said.

"Neither do I. We'll talk to each other."

"If I stay..."

"Then you'll be on the streets again."

"...maybe I'll find my parents."

"You won't have anyone if you stay and you'll be a wanderer again."

"But I'm afraid to live with Germans."

"Miriam, I think even my father is afraid to live with Germans, but the Poles don't welcome you and they don't like us either. At least you have us and we care about you. We do care about you."

Two days later, Miriam moved to Saltzheim with the Sobolov's. Their train had conductors, assigned seats and a firm schedule, delayed only by trains carrying refugees. It was early 1946 and thousands of homeless still traveled the railroad tracks of Europe. Miriam watched the passengers on these other trains, crammed into a collection of leftover freight and boxcars, which stopped at small towns for no apparent reason. The passengers were lost and empty souls, and seeing them, she knew she was right to move with the Sobolov's. In the forest, her way was to go alone but now she lived in the city, and she needed someone. The loneliness she carried was always with her, but perhaps it could be shared and the burden made lighter.

Sasha was watching Miriam watch the refugees. "Miriam, what are you thinking about when you look at these people?"

"I'm happy I'm with you and that I know where I'm going, even though I may not want to be there. But I think my family is somewhere on one of these trains."

"I wish we could be your family."

"I do too, Sasha."

They didn't talk about the refugees the rest of the trip.

CHAPTER ELEVEN

*After the liberation of the concentration
camps, survivors have no place to go.
In June of 1946, the British deny refugees
admission to displaced person camps in their
zone. By the end of 1946, the American
zones in Germany and Austria have
184,000 or 90 per cent of the survivors
in their camps.*

*Food allowance in these camps is fixed in
calories, two-thirds of which come from
bread and potatoes. The clothing allowance
is a complete set of clothes, sometimes used,
issued once a year.*

S altzheim was in Germany but the flavor of the
city was decidedly American. The Sobolov's
moved into an apartment building occupied by a
few Russian families and several American ones. Saltzheim
was more open than Disna and with spring coming, Sasha and
Miriam took daily walks through the city. Streets were
crowded with people speaking Yiddish, Polish, and Czech but
desperate questioning of Polish Jews looking for family
members was not part of the conversation.

Everyday, the two walked a kilometer to the park, past the UNNRA registration building, past the food lines, and past American soldiers. Miriam ate her first chocolate bar in Saltzheim. An American soldier walking in the park offered them the candy bar. Miriam didn't take it but Sasha did. She thanked him, and he walked off.

"You're lucky Sasha that he didn't pull you behind some trees."

Having no idea from where the comment came, Sasha said, "Really, Miriam, I don't think that's going to happen. Here take a bite."

"I don't want any."

"I'll give you half. Even my father can't get rations for American candy bars."

"Okay, I'll try it for you."

"Miriam, you're very pretty. People like to look at you when we walk so you should expect special attention."

"I don't know if I'm pretty or not. I don't think about it."

"What do you think about?"

"I wonder why we're here when Americans are everywhere. Does your father work with the Americans?"

Neither Miriam nor Sasha understood the politics of post war Europe. Germany was divided into four zones with each of the allies having control over a zone. Still, each country wanted to influence what happened in the other's zone. The Russians and the Americans fought on the same side, but didn't trust each other. After the War, they both wanted to make sure they had some control over the politics in Germany and in Europe. Each country sent representatives into the area to make friends with the Germans and to report back on political activities.

"I'm not sure what he does. I've never heard him talk about his work. Sometimes, he complains about playing this card game, shat, with Germans. He tells me about the game, but it doesn't make any sense. Even though it's a simple game, they take the bidding seriously but then play the game for fun. The deck only has 32 cards, starting with sevens and tens which are higher than kings. My father doesn't like it, but I've heard him tell my mother he plays it for political reasons."

"You mean he plays it at work."

"I'm not sure, but I don't think he plays it for fun."

"I don't understand what your father does."

"Neither do I. But I know that he doesn't want me to ask."

"Will you stay in Germany?"

"Sometime we have to go back to Russia and I hope it'll be soon. You'll like our town, Harcov."

"Does it have a registration building?"

"I don't know, but I don't think so."

"Then how will I find my family?"

"Maybe by then, you'll have made us your family."

"Sasha, I want my father to know I did it, that I listened to him. I want my mother to braid my hair and sing to me."

"If you were in Vilna at this time, without the war, you'd be making your own family. Make your family now with us. I don't want you to forget your parents. I just want you to have people around you who love you."

"I want to find them."

"Then I hope you do."

"We should stop by the UNRRA building on the way back. Since the United Nations has been keeping the lists, new names from different towns get included everyday. We can pick up the bread for your mother. You know how she hates to wait in the line."

"Miriam, I forgot the ration cards."

"Sasha, we'll go back to the apartment, and I'll get the bread on my way to UNRRA. I'll spend the afternoon waiting anyway. The lines to look at the lists are getting as long as the lists themselves."

That afternoon, Miriam didn't find a single name she recognized. Each day was the same. If she had been older when she left Vilna or if the family had lived in the city, she was sure she'd know more names.

At the bakery, she stood in a long line, humming to herself and swaying back and forth. Now, she was used to having as much food as she wanted and the flour-powdered air with the smell of dough cooking and bread cooling no longer commanded her full attention. Nor did she notice that the man behind her was listening to her quiet singing and watching her every movement.

He watched her for an hour before he said something.

"Where are you going after you get the bread?"

She didn't answer, as if she didn't hear him, and he put his hand on her shoulder. The humming stopped and the swaying stopped, but she didn't respond to his touch.

"Where are you going after you get the bread?" he repeated with a patience as if he were asking for the first time.

This time she heard, but didn't answer. Instead she asked him, "Where are you going?"

"I don't know," he said.

"I don't know either."

"You're a survivor?" he asked

"Yes."

"We don't have a place to go or a family to go home to. We should make a place with each other," he said.

"I have a home but nobody's there yet."

"You don't have a home. You know what happened."

"Some people survived," Miriam said.

"Make a home with me."

Miriam looked into the face of this man who proposed to her without knowing anything about her. She was attracted to his dark and serious eyes. In another world and in another time, she would have thought him crazy, but in this world, he was not. His black, wavy hair, almost curly, was too long for his thin face. He stooped slightly, giving him a small stomach, even though he was skinny. With more weight, he would be good-looking.

She answered as if he asked her a question about the weather. "I'm living with a Russian family. I'm using their cards to get the bread."

"I live in one of the camps, but I'm going to a kibbutz soon. I was a tailor before the war and I'm going to teach in a kibbutz that the Americans are making for us right outside Saltzheim. Then I'll go to Israel when I can. All of us in the kibbutz will go to Israel."

When he talked about being a tailor, Miriam noticed that he wasn't her age but a man already in his late twenties.

"I am serious about us making a life together."

"You don't even know my name," Miriam said.

"What is it then?"

"Miriam."

"Miriam, I'm Harry Dubinsky. I want the two of us who have nobody to have each other."

He was carrying her five loaves of bread, along with his half, when they walked out of the bakery.

"This Russian family must be important to get so many ration cards," Harry said.

"He works for the government."

"The Russian government?"

"Yes."

"In Saltzheim where all the Americans are?"

"I don't know what he does."

"He's a spy," Harry said with certainty. "I'd like to meet this Russian family. Would you arrange it?"

Miriam said yes but only because she thought Harry wouldn't leave otherwise. She gave him her name and address and then went home.

Sasha could hardly believe the story when Miriam told her.

"You met this man in the bread line and he wants to marry you?"

"He wants to make a life with me, Sasha. He has no family left, no one survived."

"You're so afraid of strangers and you talked to him?"

"He gave me no choice, the same as you. I've told him about you and he wants to meet your family."

She didn't tell her that Harry said her father was a spy.

"Will you go with him?"

"I don't think he wants to stay here, and I can't leave until I find my family. Sasha, he touched me on the shoulder and, for a second, I thought I belonged with him. He asked me to go dancing but I don't want to go."

"Why not?"

"I never danced and I don't know how. I can't even imagine people dancing in Saltzheim, not now."

"You should go if you want to see him again."

"He told me that he wants me to learn how to want things again."

"And he's right, Miriam. Go dancing with him."

The room was too small for the seven-piece band, but it made little difference because hardly anyone was dancing. An American refugee organization lent this room out once a week and the band was a volunteer group of soldiers. Harry made Miriam go to the dance floor.

"Just move the way the music tells you."

"It tells me to move to the table and sit down."

"I want you to enjoy things with me."

"Maybe, I'm not ready."

Harry liked dancing with Miriam even though they really weren't dancing together. Miriam stood still and it was only when Harry moved that her body jerked to follow. But while they were dancing, he could touch her. She didn't let him touch her, not even hold hands on the walk over, and now he was able to put his arms around her. At first, his hands fell loosely around her shoulders but as he danced, he tightened his fingers on her back.

Harry smiled at her and pressed her back for encouragement but she didn't smile back and her feet were still solid against the dance floor.

Harry kissed her on the cheek.

"I want to go home," Miriam said.

"I want you to make your home with me," Harry said.

She answered as if she took his request seriously.

"I'm not ready."

"We are like wild animals, Miriam, and we have to be normal again. I need a job and a house and a family. You need a place too. Make it with me."

Again, Miriam asked Harry to take her home.

Miriam told Sasha what Harry said and Sasha, having only met him for a few brief moments, agreed with him, but she also knew better than to argue with Miriam.

Miriam dated Harry for a month and it was after a dinner at the Sobolov's that Sasha's parents told Miriam they would like her and Harry to come back to Harcov with them and make a life there.

Harry was willing to settle in Russia if Miriam wanted it. He told her that they wouldn't have a bad life there. "Nikita Sobolov has a responsible position. He'll go back and be a state administrator because he's handled his job well here."

Even though Miriam knew the Sobolov family wanted her, she was afraid of Russia and she still didn't understand what Harry was saying about the Sobolovs. "What job, Harry?"

"Everyone is fighting over Germany, only now it's political. The Soviets want control and so do the Americans. Sobolov's job is to get to know the language, customs and politics here and then report back on the best ways to influence political organizations and elections. I told you that you were living with a spy."

"He's a good person."

"He's also a good Russian and if we go back with them, it will be a nice life as he promises."

"Harry, I'm afraid of living in Russia."

Miriam couldn't stop thinking about living in Russia. The Russians took Jacob from the farm in Vilna and now Harry was trying to talk her into moving there. She didn't understand that Harry was doing what he thought she wanted. Harry was always mixing her up and so was Sasha. She didn't need either of them. By evening, she was upset beyond reason. She left the apartment in the middle of the night and began walking, not knowing where she was going, not knowing she was walking away from Saltzheim toward the forest.

Soldiers were on the streets, even at that hour, and the ones who passed Miriam close enough to see her face offered her a place to stay for the night. When she shook her head and walked on, they didn't follow. Only one soldier grabbed her but when he felt her muscles tighten and saw her face freeze, he knew she wasn't a woman used to being on the streets in the middle of the night. He let her go with a push.

After she passed the main street, she didn't see soldiers. She didn't see anyone. She walked for an hour until the paved road became a dirt road and then a narrow path. The trees were close by. They were reaching to her.

When she walked into the forest, she was sure she would not come out. An hour later, she turned around and three hours later she was back in the apartment. Sasha was waiting.

"Miriam, you frightened me. I want to hug you but I'm too angry."

"My legs hurt and I'm cold. It was dark in the forest and I couldn't see where I was going."

"In the forest? You went into the forest?"

"The ground was covered with thick layers of dead leaves and pine needles. The wetness soaked through my shoes when I walked. Bugs were everywhere, big mosquitoes, and they bit me on the face. I couldn't move without falling over broken tree limbs and wild bushes. The trees didn't talk to me. I could hear them groaning as they swayed back and forth with the wind, but the sound scared me. I didn't know where I was going or how I would get there. I don't belong in the forest anymore."

Miriam cried, scaring Sasha because she had never seen her friend cry. She rubbed Miriam's legs to warm them and she let her cry. When the crying stopped, Sasha questioned her.

"Miriam, why did you go to the forest?"

"I don't know. I thought I'd find a place there, but I didn't. Harry wants me to go with him. You want us to go with you. I want to please you both but I want to find my family."

"Miriam, you didn't even say good-bye."

"Maybe I knew that I wasn't leaving."

"You think that you went into the forest knowing that you were coming back. Maybe you were finding out what you already knew, that just as you made a life in the forest when you had to, you should make a life outside the forest now."

"I'm very tired, Sasha. I don't want to talk anymore."

"Go to bed. Tomorrow, though, you should tell Harry what you did."

Miriam reached for Sasha's hand before she left. It was the first time Miriam had touched her.

CHAPTER TWELVE

July 1946
A quarter of a million Jews are displaced
persons in Europe. Few countries are
willing to accept them. Thousands of Jews
from Hungary and Romania start migrating
to Austria and then begin spilling over into
Italy. Jewish refugees are determined
to immigrate to a national homeland,
to Palestine.

The next afternoon Miriam went to see Harry in the makeshift kibbutz room he shared with five other men. The room was empty except for Miriam and Harry and six cots lined against the walls. The other men were in classes for the next two hours.

Harry and Miriam sat on his cot. He touched her on the shoulder as she talked and even though she flexed at each pressure, he kept his hand on her.

"Miriam, you'd better forget about the past. You need me to replace your parents and you need more. You think of yourself as a child, but you are a beautiful woman. This trip in the forest in the middle of the night showed you it's time to give up thinking about what you once needed."

"You're patient with me, Harry, like a father."

"I want to be your husband. You've got to give us a chance."

Harry stroked Miriam's arm as they talked.

"Miriam, I want you to make a decision soon. We should make plans."

Harry tickled Miriam's upper arm and moved his fingers under her sleeve. She did not let him get this close before or perhaps he hadn't thought it the right time to try. Now, he pulled his fingers from the sleeve and slid them over her blouse, gently rubbing against her breast. When he unbuttoned her blouse, she pulled backward but he didn't stop. He whispered to her all the time.

"Miriam, give us a chance. We can make a life with each other. You'll see, we'll be happy together."

He pushed her blouse aside until he could put his face into her breasts, softly rubbing his lips back and forth across her chest.

"I'll make everything up to you. I'll take care of you."

"Nobody's touched me, Harry. In the forest, nobody touched me. Once a soldier tried after the war but I didn't want him to and he left me alone."

Harry's lips slid down the center of Miriam's breasts and kissed her stomach. "I won't hurt you. I love you."

She let him caress her but she made no move to touch him. He lifted his head from her lap and reached to kiss her lips. They tightened when he pressed his lips against them. He pulled away, expecting her to reach for him but she didn't. He put his hands on her shoulders and gently pushed her down on the cot. She didn't resist but she lay there without talking, without moving. Harry bent over, kissing her forehead in soft brushing motions.

"I'll be your family. We'll have each other."

He reached to take off her blouse and then he ran his hands down her hips and legs and brought them back up under her skirt. She twisted when his hand touched her thigh but that only turned her leg into him. He didn't look at her face when he untied her skirt. For a moment, he lay next to her on the narrow cot, turning on his side to balance without leaning on her, but then he lifted himself over her and pressed gently against her.

"I can't go on unless you want me to, Miriam."

She didn't say anything but she wrapped her leg around his and slid her foot under his pants cuff. Her toes slipped under his sock and pressed against his ankle.

"Once I touched a man but his leg was metal against my hand." She mumbled the words, almost to herself, and Harry heard them only as whispers of air against his face.

The next day Miriam told Sasha she was leaving with Harry but not until she found her parents. She and Sasha were sitting on a bench in the park. Even in this city where buildings were leveled, flowers bloomed. Tulips, planted years before, were almost ready to bloom.

"You're like these tulips, Miriam. You are ready to open."

"Sasha, Harry doesn't want me talk about the past. He says talking makes it part of the present."

"It must be part of your present, Miriam. If you keep it to yourself, it'll grow inside and there won't be room for anything else to grow. You need to retell the stories and remember how well you did."

"No, Harry's right. I won't be free of the past if I keep reminding myself of it. He wants me to pledge not to talk about it anymore."

"Have you agreed?"

"I can't yet. I haven't found my parents."

"You may never find them."

"Harry says the same thing, but I can't leave without them. The lists at UNRRA are getting longer everyday and I won't give up as long as names are added."

"It could be months."

"Then it will be."

"And Harry says that he'll wait?"

"I haven't given him another choice."

"Miriam, we want you to come to Russia with us, you and Harry. My father says he could arrange a good job for Harry."

"Sasha, you've been my family since Disna. I want you to know that, but we can't go to Harcov. It's what happened to us in Poland before the Germans came. Harry and I can't forget it and we don't think the Russians want Jews."

"We want you."

"I wish it were enough."

The months that passed were uneventful. Harry continued teaching at the kibbutz, but he was losing students. They heard they could go to Austria and then, through the mountains, cross the border to Italy. The Italians didn't ask for papers and they could get to Palestine from Italy. They asked their teacher to go with them but each time he said no.

Miriam found a name of one of her father's friends, Jacob Lokovsky, on the UNRRA registration list. She spent twelve hours a day, for two days, walking the streets of Saltzheim asking about him.

On the third day, she found Jacob in a displaced persons camp on the outskirts of Saltzheim. She didn't recognize him. One of the camp administrators pointed him out and, even two feet away, she thought she had the wrong person. Her father's friend was muscular and sturdy. This man was thin and fragile.

"Jacob Lakovsky?"

"Yes."

"You're Jacob Lakovsky from Vilna?"

"Yes."

"I'm Miriam Kornitsky. You are friends with my father, Nathan."

"He had a daughter he'd take everywhere, made a tomboy out of her even though she was a beautiful girl. Was that you?"

"Yes, he taught me everything."

"I remember when they sent you away, when we heard about the Germans coming. Your father couldn't talk about it for weeks afterward. He wanted to go after you."

"Why didn't he?"

"Things got worse and worse but some of us couldn't leave our farms."

"The Germans kept you there?"

"No. We thought if we stayed, we'd have something afterwards, but if we left, they'd take it away. We didn't know the Germans; we thought they'd be like the Russians."

"Was my father there when you left?"

"I didn't leave. I was taken away. The German soldiers pulled people off the streets and from their houses and sent us to relocation camps in box cars, like animals."

"Did they take my father?"

"He wouldn't go. He fought."

"What happened to him?"

"It's not a nice story, Miriam. Maybe it's better to know that he fought them and not to know anything else."

"I have to know. You have to tell me."

Jacob Lakovsky looked at her and then, seeing her determination and her strength, he began.

"They took him in front of the village. They wanted to show us what would happen if we didn't go. They took him in front of the village and they tied him to a horse."

"On a horse?"

"No. They tied him down so that he'd have to lay behind the horse and then they whipped the horse. Even when the horse dragged him across cobblestones, he didn't cry out. Your father was a brave man. They didn't cut him loose until they knew that he was dead. They made us watch and we couldn't do anything."

Miriam didn't want to say anything, didn't want to know anymore. Still, she heard herself ask.

"And my mother, what about my mother?"

"Your mother didn't have your father's temperament. She didn't want to be strong. She would have gone with them."

"Did she?"

"Miriam, I don't want to tell you everything."

"You have to."

"Your mother is dead too."

"How do you know?"

"I know."

"Then you have to tell me how. I need to know. Did she go with them?"

"Your mother saw them kill your father. She went back to the house and hung herself. Your brother Joseph found her a few hours later. He buried both of them, under the oak tree, by the house. I was there. He didn't put down markers because the Germans would have dug up the bodies. They wanted your father to be an example. Joseph got your father's body from the street, in the middle of the night. You know everything now. I see your face and wish I hadn't told."

"My brothers went with the Germans?"

Miriam's voice was so low as not to be heard, but Jacob heard the question as if she had shouted it. He answered her because she was looking at him, needing an answer, yearning for it.

"Benjamin left shortly after you did and then Joseph went on the same train that I did, but I don't know what happened to him."

"And Jacob?"

"The same as when you left. Nathan and Rebecca did not see him again."

"Then I have no family. No family I will see again."

"I'm sorry Miriam. I'm sorry I was the one to tell."

"I'm grateful that you did."

And in some strange way, she was.

"The looking is over," she said, more to herself than to him.

That night, Miriam told Harry she was ready to leave Saltzheim.

"My parents are dead, Harry. I found out today." She told him the stories that Jacob Lakovsky told her.

The next morning when Sasha heard the stories, she cried, but Miriam did not.

"I have no reason not to start a new life, Sasha. I wanted to show my parents how well I did, what a good daughter I was. I listened to them. I went into the forest and I survived. Now, no one is left. I don't have anyone who needs to know. Harry and I are leaving for Italy tonight."

"I'll miss you Miriam."

"I won't forget you, Sasha. You saw something in a sad, sad child that no one else could see, that no one else might ever see. I want to give you something back, but I don't have anything to give. You are my family, Sasha, I know that."

The next night, Harry and Miriam left Saltzheim with ten other survivors. They hiked into Austria and made their escape through the Alps into Italy. They waded through a shallow lake to get to the Italian border and, in the middle of the water, Miriam turned to Harry and asked, "Where are we going and how will we get there?"

"We are going to Italy. From there I don't know, but we're going to take care of each other. From now on, we have no past, only a present and a future. We agree on that."

Miriam protested gently.

"Harry, my past took care of me."

They stepped from the lake into Italy.

"Maybe in the forest it did, but not now. Now, we'll take care of each other."

Miriam rubbed the gold band on her finger. She didn't want to use her parent's wedding ring in the marriage ceremony, but Harry insisted. Now, she was glad it was there to touch.

AFTERWORD

Miriam (Kenisberg) and Harry Poster lived in a displaced persons camp in Bagnoli, Italy for three years after the war. They planned to go to Palestine from Italy, but two American families sponsored them to the United States, and they came to America instead, settling in St. Louis, Missouri. While still in Italy, Miriam discovered that two of her brothers also survived the war. Both immigrated to Israel, statehood becoming official in 1948, and Miriam later travelled regularly to visit them and their children.

Physical fitness continued to be central to Miriam's life in St. Louis, as it had been in Europe. For many years, she maintained a daily exercise routine of two and a half hours in the weight room, five miles of running, one hour of roller-skating and two miles of swimming. In the coldest winters and deepest snows, she could be seen outside the St. Louis Jewish Community Center's natatorium in her bathing suit, rolling in the snow. Year round, she ran in the woods next to the JCCA, still finding pleasure in the sounds of leaves rustling and crunching underfoot as she ran through them.

Miriam used her knowledge of physical fitness to help other people, too, raising money to help the JCCA swimming program and to purchase a lift so the physically handicapped could use the pool. She also developed exercise and diet programs for disabled members of the JCCA, drawing on her own knowledge of natural cures and physical stamina.

Miriam's husband, Harry, died in 1997. And her two brothers died a few years after. Miriam slowed down in her later years, but her spirit is still strong.

For many years, she kept her pledge to Harry not to tell her story but after his death, she decided that passing on the message of her experience to young people was important. She wanted young people to know that if they work to develop a strong spirit and drive when they are young, they will be prepared to do anything, survive anything.

Miriam and
Harry Poster
in St. Louis.

Miriam Kenisberg, a young teenager, in Vilna, Poland before the War.

Miriam Kenisberg's parents in Vilna, Poland. This picture is the only one she has of them.

ACKNOWLEDGEMENTS

I want to thank people who have shared their skills and knowledge in contributing to the making and writing of this book. *Miriam's Way* has been a long time in the making, and I appreciate the patient support of everyone who helped me.

I met Miriam (Kenisberg) Poster at the Jewish Community Center swimming pool in St. Louis. She told me she had heard I was a writer, and she wanted me to hear her story. I listened, and I was moved by what she told me. Her experiences revealed details of World War II history that were new to me, and I wanted to know more. Further research confirmed for me there was a story in the forests that needed to be shared.

The story of Miriam Kornitsky, the main character of *Miriam's Way*, was inspired by Miriam Poster's true-life experiences, incorporating information I found in my research. I am grateful to Miriam for sharing her experiences and memories with me.

I am grateful to Sheldon Helfman, who helped me prepare my introductory paragraphs to each chapter, establishing the factual setting for *Miriam's Way*. Summarizing history in a few sentences is no easy task.

Mary Anne Wexler was my editor throughout the process. I want to thank her for her perseverance and her skill. The late Jeannette Eyerly, writer for children and young adults, assisted in making editing recommendations. I am grateful to students and others who read and gave comments on various manuscript drafts.

Thank you to Howard Schwartz, who gave me the confidence and support to get *Miriam's Way* published once the book was complete.

Thank you to Amy L. Davis who contributed her graphic and formatting skills, ensuring *Miriam's Way* invited readers into a dramatic story.

I am lucky to have had support and encouragement all along the way from so many friends, and I am grateful for all their efforts to help me with this project.

And for readers: I want to thank you for entering the world of *Miriam's Way*.

BIOGRAPHY

Cissy Lacks is a writer, photographer and teacher. She is a recipient of the PEN/Newman's Own Award, which is given each year to one person in the United States who has defended First Amendment rights at a personal risk. She has had several one-woman photography shows and publications in both the creative and non-fiction areas. She has a PhD in American Studies and an MS in Broadcasting. She can be reached at cissylacks@gmail.com

Made in the USA
San Bernardino, CA
18 December 2013